Greenbrier River
Mermaid

by

Rusty Mcquade

DORRANCE
PUBLISHING CO
EST. 1920
PITTSBURGH, PENNSYLVANIA 15238

Dorrance Publishing Co
585 Alpha Drive
Pittsburgh, PA 15238
Visit our website at *www.dorrancebookstore.com*

ISBN: 979-8-8868-3211-2
eISBN: 979-8-8868-3784-1

Chapter 1

Ansley's best time of the summer is sitting and looking out over the river. Smelling the sweet smells and feeling the cool air blowing through her long blonde hair. Each season of the year has its own wonderful memories for Ansley where she lives in her cabin on the Greenbrier River but summer time, when she is out of school is her favorite.

As she sat there sipping her lemonade, she looked across the river and saw something sparkling. She leaned forward to get a better look. Ansley's summer time hobby was finding treasures on the river. When the river floods and goes back down you can find many treasures.

Ansley got up, went to the river bank, and climbed into her kayak. She quickly paddled across the river and the shiny thing turned out to be an old gold necklace. She put it into her pocket and paddled back across the river.

She ran into the house shouting, "Mom, look what I found!"

Her mom looked at the necklace. "Looks like a very valuable old one. I wonder how it got there because the river hasn't been up in a while."

"I don't know," says Ansley, "But it's mine now."

"Wash up for dinner," says her mom.

"Ok," yells Ansley as she runs up to her room. She opens up her treasure box and places the necklace into it very carefully.

At dinner, Ansley says, "Dad, I now have a very old gold necklace. I found it across the river."

"That's great Ansley, now eat, we have to go to the golden hole to fish," replied her dad.

So after they finished eating, Ansley and her dad grabbed their fishing poles and a can of worms. They climbed into their kayaks and headed down the river. The sun was starting to set behind the mountain range when they get to the golden hole.

As Ansley and her dad start to fish, she asked, "Dad, do you think that necklace I found is worth something?"

"Maybe, we can take it to the jewelry store the next time we go to town," he replied.

Right at that moment, Ansley's fishing line got a tug and something was pulling the line out fast.

"Wow," said Ansley, "I've got a big one."

"Looks like it," replied her dad. "Pull it in. It's a big twelve-inch trout."

Ansley took the fish off the hook and put it in her bucket of water to keep it alive.

She yelled with excitement, "Beat that dad."

Her dad smiled and said, "I don't think I can." Ansley replies" now I know why they call it the golden hole !"

As they continued to fish from the river bank, along came Gus and Bill who have fished the golden hole for years.

"Catch anything?" they ask

"Sure did, look at the one in my bucket," replied Ansley.

"Wow, you sure did get lucky," Bill replied. "Maybe we'll get a bite or two."

Ansley and her dad started home, walking along the river trail, pulling their kayaks behind them. Ansley looked out over the river. The water was smooth and flowing quietly. Both sides of the river banks were lined with trees and the moon was starting to peep out between them.

Her dad exclaimed, "We better hurry up and get home. We have to get these kayaks put away and get these fish cleaned. Then we might have time to light a campfire along the river there at the house."

"Ok," replied Ansley, "And please, can we roast some marshmallows too?"

"Sounds good," replied her dad.

As they got closer to home, they could see the full moon coming up over the barn. The sweet smell of lilacs was in the air and they could see the fire flies dancing around the bushes. Ansley thought to herself how lucky she was to live in this beautiful place. After they put the kayaks away, Ansley's mom came out on the porch to see if they had caught anything.

Ansley said, "Hey Mom, look what I caught!" and showed her the twelve-inch trout.

"Great, that's one big fish," replied her mom. "You can clean it, your dad can fry it, and I will eat it," chuckled her mom.

They were just starting dessert when they heard a loud crack of thunder.

Ansley said, "Oh boy, a thunderstorm."

They hurriedly finished their dessert and headed out to the porch. They settled into the cozy deck chairs to watch the lightening and listen to the rain and thunder.

Finally, Mom said, "Let's all head to bed and hope that the river doesn't rise too much tonight. Also, Ansley, you probably should take a flashlight up with you in case the power goes off.."

"Good night," they all say as they headed to their bedrooms.

Chapter 2

Ansley woke up the next morning to a bright and beautiful morning. She went downstairs to the kitchen, grabbed a banana, and headed to the barn. Her first responsibility was gathering the eggs from underneath the hens. Ansley counted the eggs as she put them in the basket. Wow, twenty-two this morning. After sitting the basket on the shelf, it's time to feed all the animals their breakfast. First, she takes care of the goats and the rabbits. Next is a nice juicy apple for pixie pony since she has lots of grass in the field. Now it's time to get the grain for the chickens and ducks. The last animals to feed are the two guard dogs that live in the field to protect all the other animals. Finally, she reels out the garden hose to make sure all the animals have fresh bowls of water. After reeling in the hose, she grabbed the basket of eggs and headed back to the house to clean them and get ready for breakfast.

After breakfast, Ansley says to her mom, "I think I will head up to the train tunnel to look for Indian arrow heads."

Her mom replied, "Ok, take this bucket with you and pick some blackberries and I'll make a cobbler."

"Sounds good Mom, I'll be back by lunchtime," said Ansley and out the door she went. She jumped on her bike and up the trail she peddled toward the old train tunnel.

She was looking out over the river and saw something that made her put on the brakes hard to stop her bike. Not quite believing her eyes, she looked out over the river again and saw a big fish tail. She thought to her-self, *Wow, what a huge fish.* Then she was distracted when she heard the sound of heavy panting.

Turning around, she saw her dog Lucky and said, "Lucky, how did you get out of the barn yard?"

Lucky looked at her with his big brown eyes and wagged his tail.

"Oh alright, come on," Ansley told him as she climbed back on her bike.

The first thing she saw when she got to the tunnel was a snake. Lucky started running toward it and barking.

"No, no Lucky, that snake might bite you," yelled Ansley, "Leave it alone."

Lucky came to her and she held his collar until the snake slithered away. Thank goodness the blackberry bushes were on the other side of the trail and they are ripe. She started picking and it wasn't long until her bucket was full.

"Alright, come on Lucky, let's go in the tunnel and see if we can find some Indian arrow heads," Ansley gets to the tunnel her and Lucky go in Ansley gets her flashlight out and heads into the tunnel.

It was a good day and she found two arrowheads.

"Okay Lucky, it's getting close to lunchtime. We had better head home."

Ansley hadn't gone very far before she started smelly something fishy and Lucky was barking. She stopped her bike and looked out over the river but didn't see anything.

"Lucky, quit barking, I can't hear anything with you making all that noise,".

Ansley couldn't see anything but the fish smell was getting stronger. Just then she saw the big fish tail again as it was disappearing down under the water. Ansley thought to herself, *I really need to bring my fishing pole with me next time.* Ansley made it home in time for lunch and her mom had time to make the cobbler for dinner.

At the dinner table, Ansley told her dad about the big fish tail she had seen.

She said, "Dad, I think I'll take my pole up there tomorrow and see if I can catch that fish."

Her dad said, "Okay, but be very careful as the water is very deep at that spot and a spring feeds into the river there. You'll need to take your life jacket when you go."

After dinner, Dad started a campfire and they roasted and sometimes burned their marshmallows. The smell of the campfire filled the air, the stars were starting to twinkle and the full moon was starting to peek out over the top of the mountain range.

Ansley got up and said, "I think I'll get a jar and catch some lightning bugs." Ansley finds her jar and starts running around catching lightening bugs!

She gets back to the campfire she tells her mom and dad, "I caught twenty lightning bugs. I think that's a record."

Across and down the river they could hear the coyotes yelping. Up the river, they could hear little old man Billy playing his banjo. Life on the river was very good that evening.

Always curious about things, Ansley asked her dad, "Where does the river start?"

"Well Ansley, the east fork and the west fork of the Greenbrier rivers come together in Durbin to form this one. Then this one flows into the New River and connects with the Kanawha and Ohio Rivers. It pours into the Mississippi River and finally flows into the Atlantic Ocean."

Ansley pondered for a moment before saying, "Wouldn't it be fun to ride our kayaks all the way to the ocean?"

"I don't know how safe that would be," said her dad. "Plus, I don't have time to ride the river all the way to the ocean. It's getting late so let's get to bed. The truck is coming in the morning to stock the pond with a few fish. We have invited the local scout troop to come catch and release fish from the pond,Let s head up to bed. We have a busy day tomorrow.

Chapter 3

The next morning, Ansley woke up to her dad calling, "Rise and shine, we have to gather the eggs, feed the animals and muck out the barn."

Ansley quickly dressed and went running down the stairs, grabbed a banana and a bottle of milk.

"Hey Dad, I'll race you to the barn," laughed Ansley as she went sprinting out the door.

"Okay," answered her dad, "I'm taking the truck."

Ansley jumped on her bike and took the shortcut across the field to the barn.

"Beat you," said Ansley, after she caught her breath.

"That you did," chuckled her dad. "Ansley, grab the egg basket and gather the eggs. The first nest looked like it had a lot of eggs."

Ansley reached under the hen to get one and the hen pecked her.

"Ouch," cried out Ansley.

"Oh, Ansley," Dad said as he came over to make sure she was okay. "Leave her eggs alone. She is sitting on them and we should have some baby chickens hatching out in about three weeks."

"Wow, that is one of my favorite things to watch, baby chickens cracking out of their eggs," responded Ansley.

"Come on Ansley, let's hurry up and finish our chores. We have to get back to the house because the scouts will be arriving soon," replied her dad.

Ansley went to the shed to get her fishing pole and started toward the pond when she saw a van coming down the road. It stopped in front of the house and the scouts jumped out, all eight of them. They quickly got their fishing poles out of the back of the van.

The first thing they asked was, "Where are the worms?"

Don, Ansley's dad, replied, "Alright boys, here are the hand shovels and some cans. Go along the driveway lifting up the big rocks and you will see worm holes. Use these shovels to dig your own worms and put them in the cans with a little bit of dirt."

The boys snatched the shovels and took off down the driveway hunting for worms. As soon as they had found some worms, they went jogging to the pond, baited their hooks, and cast out their lines.

Within a matter of minutes, one scout shouted, "I caught one, look at this."

"You sure did," answered Ansley. "Now gently take it off of the hook and slowly let it loose at the edge of the pond."

The boys continued to fish for a few hours. They packed their poles back in the van, hastily changed into their swimming trunks, and raced down to the river to swim. In the meantime, Don and the scout leaders got the picnic lunch out of the van and spread it out on the picnic tables in the gazebo. Don rang the dinner bell and called for everyone to get out of the river, dry off, and come to the gazebo to eat lunch.

John, one of the scouts, said, "I bet it is awesome living here."

"Yes, it is, but sometimes the chores get to you," answered Ansley.

"What chores?" asked John.

"Well," replied Ansley, "Gathering the eggs, feeding all the animals, mucking out the barn, and helping in the garden."

"What do you do for fun?" questioned John.

"Well," responded Ansley, "I ride my bike or my pony. I fish and I swim and I paddle my kayak along the river bank looking for treasure."

"Wow, really? Treasure?" John replied. He was really curious now.

"Really," replied Ansley, "I just found a gold necklace and it's probably worth a lot of money."

Just then Jim, one of the scout leaders, said, "Okay boys, let's get in the van, it's starting to get late and we have to get back to town before dark."

"I hope to see you all again," Ansley called out, waving goodbye as the van started down the driveway. "Hey Dad, can I treasure hunt along the river for a little while?" asked Ansley.

"Sure, but don't waste time, we have chores to do before dinner," replied her dad.

Ansley went treasure hunting for a little while and didn't find anything valuable, so she headed back home. They got their chores done and went inside to eat dinner. It had been a long day and they were all tired. They quickly cleaned up the dining room table and went to bed early.

Chapter 4

The next morning, Ansley woke up to a loud *clang, clang, clang* and wondered, *What in the world is that noise?* Then she remembered that it was the bell on the front porch. Ansley hastily dressed and went running down the stairs.

"Hey Mom, what's up with the bell?" was the first thing she asked her mom.

"Your dad is at the fire pit down by the river making pancakes for breakfast," answered her mom.

"Oh boy," Ansley cried and headed toward the door.

"Ansley, please take the syrup as you go down," laughed her mom.

Ansley grabbed the bottle of syrup and scampered down the path with Lucky Dog right by her side.

"Good morning sleepy head," said her dad when he saw her coming.

"Good morning Dad, I brought the syrup," she answered.

"How many cakes do you want this morning?" asked her dad.

"Thanks Dad, I think I can eat three," responded Ansley.

Just as Ansley's dad was getting the pancakes off the griddle, her mom came down the path with the bacon and orange juice.

She said, "What a wonderful morning to have pancakes outside."

"It sure is," replied her dad. "Eat up Ansley, your cousin Rosie is coming to visit us today. After you finish eating, don't forget to go to the barn to gather the eggs and water all the animals."

As they sat there eating, they heard an eagle flying overhead and watched some wild ducks floating by on the river. Lucky Dog jumped up and headed into the water after the ducks and off they flew.

"I'm glad you are a lab and a good swimmer," giggled Ansley. "Hey, maybe we can go swimming later?" she asked her parents.

They both looked at each other and said at the same time, "After you get your chores finished."

About that time a car started down the driveway.

"Oh boy, it's Uncle Jack and he has Rosie with him."

Mom got up and started cleaning up the breakfast mess and said, "Ansley, get your basket and you and Rosie can go gather the eggs and do your barn chores."

"Sounds good," answered Ansley as she headed up the path toward the house.

Rosie jumped out of the car just as Ansley got there. She hugged her and said, "Come on Rosie, let's go to the barn."

"I'm right behind you," shouted Rosie. "Can we feed the rabbits first?" she added as they went running toward the barn.

"Ok," agreed Ansley, "Here take the rabbits these carrots, some hay, and fill up their water bowls. While you do that, I'll feed the chickens."

The girls went to work feeding the rabbits and chickens and ducks and pigeons.

"Next," said Ansley to Rosie, "Give the Pyrenees dogs two big scoops of dog food."

"Ok," replied Rosie, "And what about the pony?"

"Give her some hay," answered Ansley.

"Roger that," replied Rosie.

"Now that we've got all the animals fed and watered, it's time to gather the eggs," says Ansley.

"This will be fun," replied Rosie. "Hey, you get the eggs and roll them down the chicken coop roof and I'll catch them."

"Are you sure?" questioned Ansley.

"Yes, I can do it," giggled Rosie.

So, Ansley rolled an egg down the roof and Rosie caught it. She rolled another one and Rosie missed it, "Oops."

Then Ansley rolled another one and another one and another one. Rosie was catching some of them, but some she didn't.

The girls were laughing and having fun until, Ansley's mom Toots, yelled from the back porch, "What are you girls doing out there? We sell those eggs. Finish up and get up here to the house."

The girls quickly gather up the rest of the eggs and put them in the basket and started toward the house.

Toots is waiting for them and says, "Now you girls know better than to roll eggs off the chicken coop roof. What were you thinking?"

"Sorry Mom," Ansley replied. "We thought it would be fun."

"Well Ansley Elizabeth, I will have to take a dollar out of your egg money," replied her mom, "And Rosie, how about you wash the eggs that survived?"

"Okay Aunt Toots," Rosie replied.

"Now girls," says Ansley's mom, "When you get done, get your water bottles and your fishing poles and you can go fishing in the pond."

Rosie quickly cleaned the eggs and put them in the cartons while Ansley found the water bottles and filled them up with cold water. They go out to the shed to get their fishing poles and bikes.

"Oh wait, we have to dig some worms," says Ansley.

"Where is a good place to find worms?" asked Rosie.

"Under rocks and all those flower pots out front. Just be careful to not tip over or break the flower pots," answered Ansley.

Ansley found a bucket and they went out front to find some worms.

"How many do you think we should get?" asked Rosie.

"At least a dozen," replied Ansley.

It didn't take very long for the girls to find the worms. They grabbed their poles, climbed on their bikes, and headed toward the pond with Lucky Dog right behind them.

It only took a few minutes to get to the pond and Ansley said to

Rosie, "How about you sit on this side of the pond and I'll go to the other side so we won't get our lines tangled up?"

Just as soon as they got their lines in the water, Lucky Dog jumped into the pond.

Ansley scolded him saying, "Lucky, get out of the water. You are scaring the fish."

Lucky got out of the water, shaking himself off and slinging water all over Ansley.

Just then, Rosie jumped up and her fishing pole was bouncing.

"Hey Ansley, I got a big one and I can't hold it," she yelled.

"Hang on," shrieked Ansley, "I'm on the way to help."

At that very moment, Rosie got dragged into the pond.

Ansley was running and yelling, "Don't let go of the pole."

As soon as Ansley got there she jumped into the pond to help Rosie. With both of the girls tugging and pulling, they were finally able to get that fish dragged close to the shore. The girls were laughing so hard they were having trouble getting out of the pond.

Just then they heard Don, Ansley's dad, hollering, "You girls get out of that pond. There are snapping turtles in there. Hurry, get out now!"

The girls climbed out dragging the fish behind them and Ansley hollered, "Hey Dad, come look, we got a big one."

Dad came running to look. The first thing he said was, "That is a nice one, way to go! That's big enough to feed us all. Now you girls take it to the house so your mom can clean it."

They ran as quickly as they could lugging the fish between them to the kitchen.

"Hey Mom," said Ansley, "We caught the biggest fish in the pond."

"Wow, you girls sure did. Way to go," replied Mom. "No, oh no Lucky Dog, just look at your paws. Look at all that mud on the floor I just finished mopping," cried Mom. "And girls look at your muddy shoes and you are all dripping water all over the place."

Ansley and Rosie both said at the same time, "We will clean it up."

"Thanks girls. As soon as you finish, I have your lunch bags ready and you can eat down by the river," Ansley's mom told them.

"Great Mom, thanks," replied Ansley.

They changed clothes and working together they had the kitchen cleaned up very quickly. They grabbed their lunch bags and drinks and went to the river bank. It was a perfect day. The sun was shining brightly and the blue sky was dotted with big fluffy white clouds.

Ansley said, "Let's eat and then stretch out in our lounge chairs and watch to see what shapes we can find in the clouds."

As soon as they finished their lunch, they stretched out to cloud watch.

Ansley immediately pointed and said, "Look at that one. It looks like a dragon."

Then Rosie was pointing in another direction and saying, "Look at that one. It looks like a duck. This sure is fun living right by the river. Thanks for letting me stay for a little while Ansley."

"You're welcome," replied Ansley. "Maybe later we can ride our bikes to the sandy beach."

"What's the sandy beach?" asked Rosie.

"Well," answered Ansley, "We'll have to ride our bikes about a mile up the river trial and on the right side near the water is a big sandy place like a beach."

"Wow, that sounds so cool," says Rosie.

They lounged there a little longer letting their food settle and finding shapes in the clouds.

"Ok," Ansley jumped up and declared, "Let's go get our bikes and water bottles and go to the sandy beach."

The girls went running up the river bank and inside to get their water bottles.

Ansley's mom stopped them to ask, "what are you girls into now?"

"Well Mom, we are going to ride our bikes to the sandy beach," replied Ansley.

"Ok, take this bucket with you and pick some blackberries on the way back home and I'll make some blackberry ice cream. You girls be careful and don't get into any mischief," said Ansley's mom.

"We'll be careful," they both replied.

Ansley grabbed the bucket and out the door they raced to their bikes. They jumped on their bikes and started up the river trail.

Rosie asked, "How did this trail get here?"

"Well," answered Ansley, "It's an old railroad train track. Since this part of the county doesn't have trains running anymore, they took up all the tracks and railroad ties. They made this nice trail that follows along the river most of the time for eighty miles. Lots of people use the trail to walk or ride bikes or horses. Nothing with a motor is allowed on the trail. Stop, look over at the edge of the river. I see a big fish tail."

Rosie looked where Ansley was pointing and said, "I see it too. Wow, it's so big it looks like one of those swim fins you use when you go swimming or maybe even bigger."

"I don't know about that," replied Ansley. "There are some pretty big fish in this river and I've seen that fish tail before."

"Well, I don't see it now. We must have scared it," sighed Rosie.

"We need to get going anyway," replied Ansley. "It's just a little further to the sandy beach."

They started peddling as fast as they could to see who could get there first and they arrived at the same time. They jumped off their bikes, slipped off their shoes and went running into the sand.

"Wow, this is so cool," shrieked Rosie. "A beach out here in the mountains. Who would have guessed?"

"Yes, it is cool," replied Ansley, "And along the edge of the water we can find all kinds of colored rocks."

As they were looking for rocks the sun and sand was getting warmer so they started wading into the water.

Just then Rosie shrieked, "What is that thing going backwards and it went under a rock?"

Ansley looked and laughed and said, "It's a crawdad."

"A what?" questioned Rosie.

"Watch this," replied Ansley as she moved the rock and grabbed the crawdad behind his pinchers. "You have to be careful and pick them up behind their pinchers so their claws don't pinch you because it really hurts."

"I'm not touching that thing," shrieked Rosie. "Not for a million bucks."

So Ansley started chasing her around and around in the sand with the crawdad.

Rosie was screaming, "Please don't, get that thing away from me."

"Ok," said Ansley and she took the crawdad and put it back in the river.

They were tired after all that excitement so they went over to a big flat rock at the edge of the sandy beach and sat down. It was soothing to watch the water flow down over the rocks.

"Ansley, this whole place really is so cool," said Rosie. "The river, the sandy beach, the sun…"

"Yes, it really is cool," replied Ansley.

They drank their water and stretched out on the rock until they were dried off. Before you know it, it was time to start back home. They hopped on their bikes and started down the trail.

Before they had gone very far, Ansley stopped her bike and said, "Hey Rosie, here's the blackberry bushes."

They hopped off of their bikes, grabbed the bucket, and started picking the berries. At that moment, Rosie saw a black snake and decided to catch it right behind the head just like Ansley had caught the crawdad.

She turned around and giggling said to Ansley, "Hey, look what I have."

Ansley jumped backwards almost spilling the bucket of berries and squealed, "That's a snake, put it down."

Rosie giggled again, "It's a black snake, it won't hurt you."

"I don't care!" replied Ansley, "It's scary, put it down."

Rosie laughed and started chasing Ansley with the black snake dangling with its tail dragging the ground.

Ansley was shouting, "You won't pick up a crawdad but you'll pick up a snake? Really, put it down."

So Rosie put it down and it slithered off into the berry bushes.

"Not there," shouted Ansley.

"Why not," asked Rosie.

"Forget it, we have enough berries anyway," answered Ansley. "Let's go, it's getting late."

The girls jumped on their bikes and continued down the river trail.

"We had better hurry," Ansley said. "It looks like a storm is coming. Look at those big dark clouds."

They started pedaling as fast as they could.

They got there in the nick of time. Just as they were putting their bikes in the shed it started pouring the rain. They went running into the kitchen and gave Ansley's mom the berry bucket.

"Thank you, girls. Are the berries almost gone? I thought you would have more."

"Well Mom, someone likes to chase people around with black snakes," replied Ansley.

"Well Aunt Toots, someone likes to chase people around with craw-dads with giant pinchers," added Rosie.

"Girls, it's getting late, wash up for supper," said Ansley's mom.

The girls were hungry so they quickly washed up for dinner.

They hustled back to the kitchen and Ansley asked, "Mom, what are we having for dinner?"

"Humm," answered Ansley's mom, "we are having snake soup and crawdad salad."

"Funny Mom," Ansley replied.

Ansley's mom smiled and said, "We are having hotdogs, French fries, and macaroni and cheese with some fresh lemonade. We'll have the blackberry cobbler for dessert."

Just as they were finishing their dessert the storm moved in suddenly bringing lightning, thunder, strong winds, and heavy rain. At one point, the trees looked like they were dancing. The wind was blowing the limbs around so much that the power went off.

"No TV or internet tonight," cheered Ansley's dad, "So we can start the portable fire pit on the porch and roast marshmallows."

"Oh boy," replied Ansley, "I'll find the graham crackers, chocolate bars, and the marshmallow roasting sticks."

It didn't take long to get everything rounded up and they all went out on the porch.

Ansley's mom started to sing. *"Take me out to the ball game, take me out to the fair. Buy me some peanuts and cracker jacks. I don't care if we ever get back. So it's root, root, root for the home team. If they don't win, it's a shame. So it's one, two, three strikes and you're out of the old ball game."*

They all laugh because Mom was swinging her arms like she was trying to hit the ball.

Then they all joined in as she started to sing, *"Row, row, row your boat gently down the stream. Merrily, merrily, merrily, merrily life is but a dream."* After that they sang, "If you're Happy and you Know it, Clap your Hands". They were making so much noise and having so much fun they didn't notice that the storm was getting worse. Then they started singing If you're happy and you know it stomp your feet.

Then Rosie continued stomping around and clapping her hands and singing, "This is so much fun."

"Ok girls, the fire is ready,"shouts Ansley's dad.

Then her mom said, "Hand me the graham crackers and chocolate bars and you girls roast the marshmallows."

It only took a few seconds for them to put those roasted marshmal-lows and a piece of chocolate between two graham crackers.

"These are s'mores," mumbled Ansley. "These things are soooo good!"

"Sticky too," added Rosie. "Aunt Toots, thanks for having me over."

"No problem, Rosie. We love you and we hope you are having fun," replied Aunt Toots.

Rosie quickly replied, "I am having fun. This has been the best visit ever."

"It's getting late girls. Time to turn in, so up to bed you go," said Ansley's dad. "The storm is getting worse and who knows when the power will come back on so take these flashlights."

The girls take the flashlights and start up the stairs.

"Race you," giggles Rosie.

"You're on," replied Ansley and up the stairs they raced.

"I win," gasped Rosie trying to catch her breath.

"Only because you wouldn't let me pass you," laughed Ansley as they head into the bathroom.

They climbed into bed, got under the covers, and listened to the storm.

All of a sudden Rosie asked, "Why is your house up on stilts?"

"Well, sometimes the river flood waters get so high that the water comes all the way up here to the house. The house is on stilts so the water doesn't come into the house. Sometimes the water gets into the barn though because the creek is on one side and the pond is on the other."

Just then there was a streak of lightning that lit up the room and a crack of thunder that made the windows rattle.

"Wow, that one was really loud," whispered Rosie.

The girls laid there for a while just listening to the rain beating down.

"This is going to be a bad one," whispered Ansley back.

"Good night," yawned Rosie.

"Good night, don't let the bed bugs bite," replied Ansley.

"What, do you have bed bugs?" asked Rosie.

"No," laughed Ansley sleepily, "That's just an expression."

The girls finally fell asleep.

Chapter 5

*C**lang, clanggg, clanggggg!*
Rosie jumped straight up in the bed and almost fell out.

"What is that noise it's not even 6:00 AM yet?" she squealed.

Ansley quickly replied, "Get up and get dressed. Something must be horribly wrong. That is the warning bell on the front porch."

The girls quickly got dressed and went running down the stairs.

"Hey Mom, what's going on?" asked Ansley.

"The river is already out of its banks and it's still rising," replied her dad. "Girls, quickly get your bikes up on the porch and secure the kayaks. Then go to the barn and get all the animals to the upper field beside the river trail."

"Okay Dad," replied Rosie. Then she asked, "Dad, where is Lucky?

"I haven't seen him this morning. He's probably at the barn. Now hurry girls, we have a lot to do," he responded.

The girls ran to the shed and got the bikes and put them on the porch. Then they ran under the house and secured the kayaks to the posts. In the meantime, Ansley's dad moved the lawn movers and the tractor to the upper field.

Just then Ansley's mom called, "Girls, come and put on your water-proof wading boots. The river is still rising and the pond is starting to overflow into the field. The water is almost to the barn."

They quickly took off their tennis shoes and put on their waders.

Then they ran to the barn and put a halter on the pony and ropes around the necks of the three goats. Rosie and Ansley hurriedly left the barn leading the pony and goats with the chickens and ducks following behind. They turned them loose in the upper field and went running back to get the rabbit cages and saw the white homing pigeons were gathering on top of the barn.

The whole time Ansley is calling, "Lucky, Lucky, where are you?"

At that very moment, he came running out of the barn where he had been snuggled up in the hay.

"There he is," yelled Rosie.

He was running right behind the geese.

Ansley scolded him saying "Lucky, don't chase the geese in the wrong direction. We are trying to get all the animals to the upper field."

At that very moment, Lucky slipped and fell into the high, muddy water. He kept trying to swim back to shore but the current was carrying him further away.

"Rosie," shouted Ansley, "Let's get the canoe."

They quickly grabbed their life jackets and started dragging the canoe toward the river. When they got to the edge of the water they jumped in the canoe and start paddling toward where Lucky had fallen into the water.

"There, over there," Ansley points toward Lucky.

His head is bobbing up and down in the strong current but his front legs are popping up out of the water with every stroke he was taking.

"Lucky, Lucky, we're coming to get you," Ansley shouts.

She wasn't paying attention to the river and a log struck the canoe hard. Out flew Rosie and then Ansley. They are in a narrow part of the river and the water is rising and the current is swifter.

"Try to keep your feet pointed downriver," shouts Ansley to Rosie.

Ansley's mom came out on the porch just in time to see them flying out of the canoe.

She immediately screamed, "Don, Don, the girls are in the river."

"Ohhhh my heavens," he gasped. As soon as he recovered, he yelled,

"Girls, keep your feet downriver and your heads up. I'll get the truck and head toward the bridge over the river." He jumped in the truck, gunned the engine, and went spinning down the gravel road.

Rosie is slowly getting closer to the shore but Ansley was still concentrating on getting to Lucky. About that time the raging current tossed her up and when she came down her head struck a rock.

Rosie saw what happened and started screaming, "Ansley, Ansley answer me. Are you ok?"

There was no answer. Rosie grabbed a low hanging tree branch and was able to hold on. She could see Ansley's life jacket bobbing up and down as Ansley went floating down the river. She was so scared and didn't know what to do. Should she let go and go try to save Ansley?

At that very moment, she heard someone shout, "Hold on and I'll get a rope."

Farmer Workman ran and got a rope and tied a big ring on the end of it. He threw it out above where Rosie was hanging on and told Rosie to grab hold of the ring when it floated to her. Rosie reached for the ring when it came to her.

Farmer Workman called, "Now, let go of the branch and grab the ring with both hands. Hold on tight and I'll pull you in. That's a good brave girl, almost there." As soon as she was safely on shore, he asked, "Girl, why were you in this river?"

"Well, my cousin Ansley's dog Lucky fell in and we were trying to save him," she answered him through chattering teeth.

"And where is Ansley?" asked Farmer Workman.

"She's still in the river," replied Rosie.

Farmer Workman sprang into action. "Come on, we'll head down river on my four-wheeler. Wrap this blanket around you and jump on the back."

As they were rounding the last turn in the road, they saw Ansley's dad had just gotten there. He jumped out of the truck when they came skidding to a stop right beside him.

"Have either of you seen Ansley?" asked her dad.

Rosie whimpered, "Not since I saw her hit her head on a rock. Dear God, where is she?"

"Don't worry, we will find her," encouraged farmer Workman.

Ansley's dad raised his head and said, "Rosie, you stay here on the bridge and keep your eyes on the river. If you see Ansley blow this fog horn."

"Alright Uncle Don, I can do that," she replied.

Farmer Workman said, "I'll cross the bridge and head back up the river bank."

Ansley's dad said, "Ok, I'll take the truck and go back up the bank on this side."

Chapter 6

Ansley's dad and Farmer Workman slowly and carefully started searching both sides of the river.

Meanwhile, Ansley slowly opened her eyes and was looking up at the sky. At first, she didn't know where she was and wondered if she was having a dream. She felt her body floating out of the water toward a big rock and being pushed up like something was lifting her. She was finally able to climb on to the top of the rock and safely out of the water. She looked around and didn't see Rosie. Then she remembered Lucky Dog and started yelling for him. But there was no sign of either of them.

Then, still as if in a dream, she heard, "Ansley, don't move in case you slip off the rock back into the water."

It was so good to hear her dad's voice she almost jumped off the rock.

"Dad, Dad, where's Rosie?" she asked.

"She's ok," he called back, "she's waiting on the bridge."

"What about Lucky Dog?" was her next question.

"I'm sorry Ansley, we haven't seen any sign of him," he sadly replied.

Ansley turned over on her belly, hid her face and started to cry.

"Ansley, please don't move, I'm going for help to get you off that rock. Then we'll look for Lucky," encouraged her dad.

He jumped in the truck and headed to the nearest house.

He got there in just a few minutes, jumped out of the truck and shouted, "Hey Gus, do you have any good strong rope? Ansley is stuck on a rock in the middle of the river about a mile upstream."

Gus went running to his shed yelling as he went, "I sure do and a life ring too."

Gus grabbed the rope and ring and jumped in the passenger seat of the truck. Don quickly turned the truck around and he and Gus headed back to where Ansley was stuck on the rock.

When they pulled down to the water's edge where Ansley was now sitting up, she yelled, "Dad, I see Lucky. He's lying on the shore behind a rock right down from where you are. Please go get him."

Ansley's dad called back, "We'll get you first."

He threw the ring out, but missed the rock where Ansley was sitting. The river was very wide and the water was still raging. It took both men to get the ring pulled back in. This time they both threw it, but it still didn't reach Ansley. They try again and again.

Finally, Ansley was able to grab the ring.

"Now put the ring over your head and pull it down to your waist."

They tied their end to a tree just to be extra careful.

"Hold onto the rope as tight as you can and we'll pull you safely in."

Ansley did as he instructed and both men start to pull as Ansley slid off of the rock. They were struggling to get her to shore so she started kicking her feet with all her might to help. They finally got her pulled safely to shore and her dad grabbed her up and hugged her like he was never going to let her go.

Then he put her down and asked, "Ansley, what in the world were you thinking?"

"Dad, Lucky fell in and you know he's not the best swimmer. You know he's my protector and I don't know what I would do without him. Come on, let's go get him," cried Ansley as she went running toward Lucky.

When she got to him, she was relieved to see that his side was moving.

"Oh Dad look, he's breathing," she cried. Then she turned to her dad and asked, "Where's Rosie?"

He replied, "She's on the bridge with the foghorn watching for you, so we better go get her."

He gently picked up Lucky, carried him to the truck, and laid him in the back of the truck. Ansley climbed in the back and laid Lucky's head in her lap. Gus climbed in the passenger seat. Don jumped in the driver's seat and they headed toward the bridge.

When he stopped the truck Rosie came running, crying, and shouting, "Where's Ansley? Where's Ansley?"

Ansley popped her head up out of the back of the truck. She yelled, "I'm here in the back with Lucky."

Rosie jumped in the back of the truck with Ansley and the girls hugged and didn't want to stop.

Ansley's dad called back to them, "Set down girls, we've got to get Lucky Dog to the vet."

They started out the gravel road toward the main road and it was flooded over.

"What now?" asked Gus.

"We'll have to get up on the river trail. It's on higher ground," replied Ansley's dad.

This is an emergency so he drove the truck up to the crossing and pulled onto the trail. They looked down at the muddy brown rolling river. Logs and debris were bobbing and floating along.

"Hey, there goes a lawn chair," pointed out Ansley.

"Oh, look there goes a gas tank," chimed in Rosie.

As they start up the trail, they see what looked like a porch railing-floating down river.

Ansley's dad sighed, "It's stopped raining so the river will crest soon, I hope."

It didn't take long to get to the vet's office. Don pulled into the parking lot and blew the horn.

Julie, the vet, came running out and asked, "what's the matter?"

Ansley called from the back of the truck, "It's Lucky. He fell in the river and he's unconscious."

Julie checked him and said, "He's alive for now. Let's get him inside."

Don and Gus gently picked him up and carried him inside.

Julie took his vitals and said, "I'll do what I can, but it will probably take a while."

"Ok, please let us know if there are any changes," replied Ansley's dad.

Ansley pleaded, "Dad can't we wait? I don't want to leave Lucky."

"No, we have to get Gus home and get to the house and check on all the animals," replied her dad.

Julie assured Ansley that she would call with any updates.

As they were getting in the truck Julie hollered, "Good luck folks, the river is still coming up."

"I know," answered Ansley's dad. "Jump in everyone, we better hurry up."

They quickly started back down the trail. It seemed a little bumpier since they were going faster. They dropped off Gus and he hopped out of the truck.

He hollered, "Good luck, call me if you need me."

"Thanks neighbor, I will," replied Ansley's dad.

As they head on down the trail, they could see that the water was still rising.

Don pulled off the river trail and stopped the truck safely in the driveway. "We're here girls. Let's get into the house."

Ansley's mom met them on the porch. After she hugged them, she said, "You girls get those boots off, go get cleaned up and I'll have supper ready when you get back downstairs."

"Ok," answered Ansley.

Rosie chimed in, "I see the water running under the house. I understand now why your house is up on stilts."

The girls showered and put on some warm clean clothes. They went running downstairs and they all sat down to eat and talk about everything that had happened that day. Then they moved in to the living room to relax and watch the news.

Rosie looked around and asked, "What do we do now?"

"Wait," answered Ansley.

Chapter 7

As they watched the sun setting behind the mountains, they could see that the water was finally starting to go down.

"Wow," sighed Rosie, "So much water and it came up so quickly!"

The girls walked out onto the porch and sat down to watch the rolling water rush by.

"Look," cried Ansley, "A whole tree. Roots and all."

"Yikes," cried Rosie, "There goes a canoe and no one is in it."

"Yep," replied Ansley. "They didn't get it tied up very well. Just wait until tomorrow after the water goes down. We will find all kind of treasures." Ansley looked at Rosie and said, "I need to tell you something."

"What?" questioned Rosie.

"Well, while I was in the river tumbling around and trying to stay afloat, something underneath me lifted me up and helped me keep my head out of the water," answered Ansley.

"Oh, probably just a log," said Rosie.

"No way, it lifted me up out of the water and halfway pushed me onto that big rock," replied Ansley.

"Maybe it was Big Bart the fish," laughed Rosie in a way that you knew she didn't believe Ansley.

"Rosie," demanded Ansley, "I'm telling you the truth! Something saved my life."

"Well, thank God you were saved," said Rosie trying to change the subject.

"I'm going to figure out what it was," answered Ansley with determination.

"How are you going to do that?" joked Rosie.

"I'll paddle my kayak up and down the river until I figure it out," replied Ansley very seriously.

Rosie still didn't quite believe her and giggled, "Maybe it was an alligator. Good thing it didn't eat you."

"You are NOT funny," snapped Ansley.

Ansley's dad came out on the porch and asked them, "What are you girls talking about?"

Rosie replied, "We are thanking God that the alligator didn't eat Ansley."

"What, there are no alligators in these waters," said Ansley's dad, shaking his head.

"Dad, Rosie is just teasing me," giggled Ansley. "I told her that I felt something lift me up and push me toward the rock I was on."

"Well, I'm glad you made it safely onto that rock," replied her dad.

Before Ansley could try to convince her dad that something did help her on to the rock, they heard the phone ringing and went rushing into the house.

Ansley's mom had already answered the call and was saying, "Hello." Then after listening for a few minutes, she slowly said, "Yes, I understand. Thank you and yes, I'll let Ansley know."

After hanging up the phone, she turned to Ansley and said, "That was Vet Julie and she wanted to let us know that Lucky Dog has several broken bones and a head injury. He is still hanging in there but he may not make it through the night."

It had been a long traumatic day and Ansley broke down and started crying.

After a few tears she said, "Mom, he'll pull through this. I know he will, he has to make it. He's my buddy." She went over and fell on the sofa and continued to cry.

Rosie tried to comfort her and soothingly saying, "Ansley, he's a tough dog. Sit up and we will pray for him."

After she had calmed down her dad said, "Come on girls, we have to go check the barn."

Ansley got up with determination, wiped her face and announced, "Rosie you are right. Lucky is a tough dog and we do have chores that have to get done."

They walked out the road toward the barn and saw that most of the field was still covered with at least three feet of water. The Pyrenees dogs, pony, and the two goats are in the upper corner of the field on higher ground. They see the chickens are over in the neighbor's yard and the ducks are playing in the water. The rabbits are in their cages on the higher platform and the white pigeons are still on the barn roof.

Ansley cried out, "Oh, no, two of the chickens must have tried to get back in the barn to roost and drowned."

"Take them to the corner of the upper field and we will bury them later. It's getting too dark to do it this evening," replied her dad.

Rosie asked, "Is the water still rising?"

Her uncle replied, "No, it is slowly going down. See that high water mark on the barn where the wood is still wet

They walked closer to the barn to make sure all the animals were safe for the night.

As they started toward the house, the lights in the house went off.

"Oh great, no power again," remarked Ansley.

Her dad took a flashlight out of his pocket and responded, "I was afraid of this."

As they walked into the house, her mom was lighting some candles.

She immediately asked them to help her, "Hey Don, would you fill the kerosene lamps with fluid and girls help me round up some more candles. Then we will settle down and have some dessert."

While the girls were helping Ansley's mom with the candles, her dad went out on the porch and carried in an armload of firewood and started a fire in the fireplace. Before they knew it, the house was softly glowing from the light from the candles, the lanterns and the fireplace.

"Well, this is really cozy. Let's have some chocolate chip cookies and milk," suggested Ansley's mom.

"OK" cried the girls while her mom and dad chuckled.

"Look what I found while I was looking for the lanterns," said Ansley's dad as he pulled his guitar out of its case. "Do you gals want to sing some cowboy songs?" he asked.

"Yippee," they said in unison.

Ansley wanted him to play "Oh, Susanna" and Rosie asked for "She'll be Coming Around the Mountain when She Comes".

He started playing and they all sat around the fireplace singing songs one after another until he finally said, "That's enough for tonight. My fingers are sore and it's getting late. We better head to bed. It'll be time to get up before you know it."

The girls started up the stairs and Ansley stopped and said, "Wait Rosie, we had better go to the bathroom first."

"But where?" asked Rosie.

Ansley chuckled and replied, "We will have to go outside.,"

Rosie questioned, "Are you kidding me?"

"Nope," replied Ansley, "Here's some toilet paper and a flashlight. I usually go across the driveway behind one of those big trees when the power is off."

"I've changed my mind," quivered Rosie, "I don't have to go after all."

"Suit yourself," answered Ansley, "But in the middle of the night when you really have to go is when the coyotes come out. So you had better go now."

"Ok, if you are serious," she replied.

Both girls grabbed some toilet paper and they went flying out the door and down the porch steps.

Ansley started laughing and taunted Rosie, "Maybe the alligator will get you."

"Ha, ha," joked Rosie, "If it didn't eat you, it won't eat me."

The girls went behind two trees and used the bathroom as fast as they could. Then they went racing back to the house and up the stairs to the porch. They hurried on into the house and used wipes to clean their hands.

Ansley's dad was putting away his guitar when they came in. He looked around and said, "Bedtime girls. We will have a lot of extra work to do tomorrow."

They went upstairs and quickly changed into their nightgowns and climbed into bed.

Rosie asked, "What did your dad mean when he said we will have extra work to get done tomorrow?"

"You'll just have to see it to believe it. The high water always brings treasure but it also brings trash," sighed Ansley.

Chapter 8

The next morning, they woke up to the sun shining in the window and they could hear birds singing and the rooster crowing.

"Finally," Ansley cheered with delight, "The storm is finally over."

Rosie jumped up and looked out the window. "Oh my, look at all that mess. Tree branches, all kinds of cans and bottles and lots of mud and rocks. Look, part of the fence is leaning over and your dad is trying to get it standing straight up again using the tractor."

Ansley jumped up too and said, "Well, we had better get dressed and head downstairs. It's going to be a long day."

They hurried downstairs and grabbed a breakfast bar and a glass of milk.

Ansley's mom came in from feeding the cats on the porch and said, "Here are your barn boots girls."

They put them on and headed to the barn to check on the animals. The dogs, goats, pony, rabbits, ducks, and pigeons were all accounted for. Then they started trying to find all the chickens.

"Oh no," cried Ansley. She found four more dead chickens crammed in a corner halfway covered with debris.

"That's a shame," said Rosie. "That makes six that we will have to bury."

"Oh no," cried Ansley, "That's my favorite rooster, Punky."

Punky was a black rooster with long white feathers on his head that hung down like a punk rocker. She began to whimper as she picked up Punkie.

Rosie hugged her and said, "I'm sorry about Punky. What do you think happened?"

Ansley replied, "Maybe they were already asleep on the roost and the water slowly crept over them and they couldn't escape. You can see where part of the roost was underwater. We'll have to put Punky and the other three chickens out with the other two and bury them later. Right now, we have to get this mess cleaned up so the rest of the animals won't get sick."

Don had left some bales of straw for the girls to put down fresh bedding for the animals. Before they could do that, they had to muck all the wet hay and bedding out of the barn. They shoveled and raked and wheel barrow at least thirty loads of wet soggy mess out of the barn before it looked ready for them to spray disinfectant. Then they wheeled the bales of fresh straw in. They started with the Pyrenees dogs, Jackie and Livy. Fresh bedding, fresh water, and fresh food. Next came fresh bedding, water, and food for the goats and the pony. Then came the chickens and ducks and pigeons. They got the rabbit cages down off of the platform, cleaned up their hutch and put in fresh food and water and got them safely back in. So far, so good. Finally, all the animals had clean beds, food and water. They had been working non-stop all morning so they headed toward the house to clean up and eat some lunch.

Rosie was washing her hands and said, "Look, I have a blister."

Ansley looked down at her hands and replied, "Yep, me too."

Ansley's mom called from the kitchen, "Hustle up girls, lunch is ready. We're having soup and sandwiches."

"Great! We're hungry," they both answered at the same time.

Her dad came in just as they were sitting down. He quickly cleaned up and sat down.

The first thing he said was, "Everyone, eat a good lunch because we have more work to get done. The good news is I got the fence fixed. The bad news is the tractor is broken."

Her mom asked, "How long do you think it will take to get it fixed?"

Her dad said, "I don't know. I'll have to go to town to get parts first. This afternoon we'll just hook the cart behind the lawnmower and I'll worry about the tractor another day."

Just as they were clearing the table the phone rang. Ansley's mom answered the phone. They heard her say, "Ok, that really sounds encouraging. I'll let Ansley know." She hung the phone up and turned around with a big smile. "That was the Julie the Vet and she called to let us know that Lucky made it through the night and he is drinking water this morning."

"Thank God," exhaled Ansley's dad.

Ansley added, "Way to go Lucky, I knew you'd make it. Can we go see him?"

Both of her parents said at the same time, "Tomorrow. Right now, we have lots more work to get done today. Let's try to get the yard cleaned up."

They all head outside.

Ansley's dad said, "The best way to get rid of all these leaves and branches is to haul them to the river and let them keep going downstream. Anything that's trash we'll pile up and send to the dump."

"Wow," remarked Rosie, "The river is still pretty high and very muddy."

"Yes, but it's going down and that's what matters," replied Ansley's dad. "It will take us weeks to get everything straightened back up."

They were cleaning up the mess that had accumulated under the house when they heard the water pump kick on.

"Yippee," they all cried in unison, "The power just came back on."

Ansley's mom said, "You guys clean a while longer out here and I'll go inside and fix us a nice warm dinner."

When they sat down for dinner and said a prayer of thanks, Ansley's mom uncovered a platter of grilled hamburgers and all the fixings, potato salad, and a chocolate cake for dessert.

Rosie piped up and said, "This is great, now I can pee in the toilet and won't have to go outside behind a tree."

They all just busted out laughing.

After dinner they all went out on the porch to relax and eat watermelon. They started talking about the state fair and what they enjoyed the most.

"My favorite thing is the rides," said Rosie with excitement.

"I love the horse shows the best," added Ansley.

Her mom added her favorite was the food, "You don't have to cook it or clean up the mess."

Her dad added without hesitation, "Mine is the tractor pulls. Plus, it is always a good way to learn what the newer model tractors have to offer."

As they sit and talk and listen to the river rushing by, they reflect how thankful they are that the water didn't get any higher or cause any major damage.

The sun had barely set behind the mountain when Rosie said, "I'm really tired."

Ansley agreed and added, "Let's head to bed."

It didn't take long for them to brush their teeth and get changed. They were both wore out and were asleep as soon as their heads hit their pillows.

Chapter 9

The sound of the phone ringing woke them up early the next morning. Ansley's mom answered the phone and then they heard her loud and clear, halfway crying, "Oh my God, oh my God, oh my God."

Then they heard Ansley's dad saying, "Toots, what's the matter?"

Hanging up the phone she started sobbing, "Rosie's mom and dad were out on their boat in the gulf when this storm hit. They just found their boat, but no one was on it."

Rosie heard this as well and come rushing down the stairs shouting, "What, what, what did you say Aunt Toots?"

Just as Ansley got downstairs her mom was saying, "Rosie, I know this is shocking news, but calm down. They already have rescue workers out searching for them and they promised to keep us updated."

"I told them not to go! I begged them to stay here in the mountains!" cried Rosie.

"Rosie, they will find them," Aunt Toots said as she hugged Rosie. "We need to pray and keep ourselves busy. Now let's get ourselves focused and eat this nice breakfast I've prepared before it gets cold. Then you girls can go to the barn and double check all the animals to make sure they are still doing ok. That storm was traumatic for them also. Then get them all fed and watered. Here's the basket for the eggs."

As soon as they finished eating, Ansley jumped up and said, "Come on Rosie let's go."

They both put on their barn boots and headed toward the barn. As soon as they got there Rosie sat down on a hay bale and started to cry. Livy, the white Pyrenees dog came trotting over and put her head in Rosie's lap. Rosie immediately put her arms around Livy's neck and hugged her like she would her parents.

Rosie murmured into Livy's ear, "It will be ok, won't it Livy?"

Livy looked up at her, barked, and went running into the barnyard. Rosie felt better, got up, grabbed a shovel and started cleaning out the pony's stall.

In the meantime, Ansley was taking care of the rabbits.

She heard Rosie shouting, "No, no, get away."

Ansley went into the pony's stall to see what was going on. There was Rosie backed into the corner and the big red rooster was standing in front of her.

"It's ok Rosie, that's Pretty Boy. He won't hurt you. He just wants his bread treats. I give him pieces of stale bread and he thinks he's special," giggled Ansley.

She walked over to a shelf and got some pieces of bread and tossed one to Pretty Boy.

"Here Rosie, you try it," instructed Ansley and Rosie tossed a piece. "Now hold a piece out and watch what he does."

Pretty Boy strutted up and took that piece of bread right out of her hand just like a dog would do.

"That's cool," laughed Rosie so she fed the last few pieces to him. Then for their special treats, they fed all the chickens some meal worms, the ducks some lettuce, the pony an apple and the rabbits some strawberries.

"Now," Rosie, "If you will grab the egg bucket, we will gather the eggs."

They gathered the eggs and placed them all gently into the bucket. They cleaned out the wading pool so the ducks would have some fresh water to play in. Ansley had the water hose and was refilling the pool when Rosie came around the corner of the barn.

Ansley cries, "Rosie, lookout," just as Rosie slipped in a big patch of mud and down she went.

Both girls started laughing as Rosie was trying to get up and kept having trouble getting up in the slippery mud.

Ansley joking said, "Rosie, a lot of women pay big bucks for a mud spa treatment and you are getting one for free."

Rosie decided that Ansley needed a treatment too so she picked up a handful of mud and hit her with it. Ansley was still holding the water hose and water was spraying all over the place. When Ansley turned around to turn it off, she fell in the mud as well. They both looked at each other all covered in mud and just sat there laughing. The pony, Pixie came out of the stall and just stood there staring at them. The girls managed to slip, slide and scoot to drier ground and finally got up.

The water was still spewing out of the water hose so Ansley pointed it up in the air and they danced around underneath the makeshift shower and rinsed off all the mud. Ansley turned off the water hose while Rosie grabbed the bucket of eggs they headed toward the house. Just as they walked up the steps of the porch Ansley's mom stepped out of the house, took one look at them and busted out laughing.

"Well girls, I'm not sure I want to ask what you've been into this time," was the first thing she said. Then, "I'll go get some soap and some towels. The water has cleared up so you girls head to the river and get cleaned up."

The girls walked into the river until it was almost up to their waist. They soon realized they still had quite a bit of mud on them.

Ansley said, "Hey Rosie if I turn around will you scrub my back? Then I'll do yours."

When she turned around, she was looking out over the river and she saw something that looked like a fish tail.

"Look Rosie, there's that big fish tail," shrieked Ansley.

"Where?" asked Rosie, "I don't see anything."

"Right there beside that rock," answered Ansley.

"I still don't see anything," replied Rosie.

"Forget it now," Ansley responded. "It went under the water, around the island, and disappeared."

At that very moment, they heard Ansley's mom calling, "What are you girls doing? Hurry up, your lunch is ready."

They finished washing up, hopped out of the river, grabbed their towels, and quickly dried off.

They ran up the steps and hurried into the bathroom to change clothes. Then they went hurrying into the dining room.

Ansley suddenly realized that she was hungry and asked, "Mom, what's for lunch?"

Her mom came in with a big round pan and said, "Would anyone like pizza for lunch?'

"Oh Mom, that sounds fantastic," Ansley quickly replied.

"You are the best Aunt Toots," Rosie quickly added.

They were getting ready to sit down when they heard a loud noise that came from across the river.

"I wonder what that was," said Ansley and all three of them went running out to the porch.

Ansley's dad was coming up the steps and he said, "I'm pretty sure one of the trees on the island just fell. I figure all that water damaged the roots."

"Man, it must have been a big one from the sound of that crash," responded Rosie.

"Yep, I agree with that," answered Ansley's dad. "Now let's go eat, something smells mighty good."

Just as they were settling down at the table the phone rang.

Ansley's mom got up and answered it. "Hello, yes, okay, I understand, okay, I'll talk to Don and we'll get back to you."

"What was that all about?" Don asked after she hung up the phone.

"Well, the rescue team needs more help," replied Toots. "They want to know if you will fly down to help."

Don thought for a minute and said, "Let's talk about it while we eat lunch."

After a few minutes he said, "If you girls can handle all the chores I will go, the quicker they are found, the better."

Toots quickly answered, "The girls and I will be fine. If we need any help, we can call one of the neighbors. I'll help you pack while the girls clean up the table."

Rosie said, "I want to go help look for Mom and Dad."

"No, Rosie, I need you to stay here and help on the farm," firmly replied her Uncle Don. "There will not be any other kids there and I would never forgive myself if anything happened to you. I'll call you all as soon as I get there with any updates."

Rosie knew that her Uncle Don was right and it would be best for her to stay with her Aunt Toots and Ansley. She was still a little sad so her and Ansley went outside to eat some watermelon while her aunt and uncle dashed around packing his bag. He needed to leave soon if he was going to catch the last flight out of the day.

He came out of the house carrying his suitcase and hugged Toots and the girls and said, "I love you all and I hope to see you soon."

Toots and the girls stood at the edge of the driveway as he hopped into the truck and they waved until he went out of sight.

The rest of the afternoon seemed to drag by. Rosie and Ansley rushed to get their evening chores done so they could get back to the house in case the phone rang. Finally, dinner was finished and no phone calls so they decided to have a movie night. They popped some popcorn and as they ate it, they watched a scary movie. It was getting pretty late and they started up the stairs to get ready for bed.

Rosie turned around and said, "Aunt Toots, please wake me up when Uncle Don calls."

"I will," replied Aunt Toots.

The girls brushed their teeth, changed into their sleeping clothes and climbed into bed.

As soon as Ansley turned off her light Rosie asked, "Why did they call your dad to help with the rescue."

"I think because he was the Coast Guard director for the Kodiak,

Alaska rescue swimmers. They are some of the highest honored ser-vicemen," answered Ansley. "If anyone can find them, Dad can do it."

Rosie said, "That's good to know," as she turned off her light.

"Don't worry, they will find them. Just wait and see. Good night, now try to get some sleep," murmured Ansley as she was already drifting off.

"Good night to you too, Ansley," whispered Rosie.

Chapter 10

Early the next morning the warm sunshine streaming through the window was hitting Rosie on the face and it woke her up. She laid there for a while enjoying the sounds from the river and the birds singing. She was thinking about her mom and dad and hoping that Uncle Don would call with good news. She was also thinking about what her parents would say, "Pray anytime you are troubled." So Rosie prayed for her parents and that the rescue workers would soon find them. She felt much better and knew that they were okay. But the longer she laid there thinking about all the possibilities, the seeds of doubt started creeping in. The next thing she knew she was crying.

The sniffling woke Ansley up because she turned over, looked at Rosie and asked, "Are you ok?"

"Yes, I'm ok," replied Rosie in between sniffs. "I was just thinking about Mom and Dad and worrying because we haven't heard anything."

Ansley said with great confidence, "Don't worry, they will find your mom and dad. My dad is the best at search and rescue."

"I sure hope so. It just seems to be taking a long time," murmured Rosie between sniffs.

Suddenly, Ansley jumped up out of bed and jumped up and down clapping her hands. "Hey Rosie, I know what will make you feel better. Come on, let's get up and get dressed. Today we are going to town. We are entered in the lightening bug contest. We will have to hurry up and decorate our pickle jars."

Ansley's mom called up to them just then, "Come on down girls. The eggs are ready and the bacon is almost ready. I need you all to make the toast."

"Ok Mom, we're almost ready," answered Ansley.

They quickly finished dressing and started down the steps. They were on the last step when the phone rang.

Ansley picked up the receiver and said, "Hello. Yes, we will be in town today. Then, that's great. Thanks for letting me know." She hung up the phone and went running into the kitchen yelling, "Mom, Mom, that was Vet Julie. She called to let me know that Lucky is eating, drinking and doing much better so we can stop by to see him today."

"That's good news.," replied Ansley's mom. "Let's eat and get our chores done. Then we will head into town."

Rosie and Ansley finished their breakfast and headed straight to the barn.

"Hey Rosie, how about you gather the eggs and I will water all the animals?" offered Ansley.

"Sounds like a plan," replied Rosie. Then she asked, "Can I give the pony an apple?"

"Sure," answered Ansley, "And give the rabbits some lettuce leaves please."

"Ok," answered Rosie.

The girls finished their chores in record time and started back to the house.

They were running up the porch steps when Ansley's mom came out on the porch.

She said, "Rosie, your Uncle Don called to let us know they found two more survivors and they are still looking for your mom and dad. Hang in there and don't lose hope."

What her Aunt Toots didn't tell Rosie was that they had found four people dead.

She opened the door and said, "Come on girls, let's go paint our pickle jars, head into town and see Lucky before we go to the picnic."

"Ok," answered both girls.

They painted stars and flowers on their jars, jumped in the truck and headed to town.

As soon as Ansley's mom stopped the truck in front of the vet's office, the girls jumped out and went running inside.

Vet Julie said, "Hello girls, come in. Lucky is ready for visitors."

As they turned the corner there was Lucky in a big dog cage wagging his tail.

"Lucky is eating and drinking normally. He has a broken leg and I had to put on a cast. I need to keep him a while longer for observation. Other than that, he's fine and should be able to go home in a couple more days."

In the meantime, the girls hug Lucky as he is licking them up and down.

"Oh, Lucky, I love you sooo much," Ansley tells him.

"Me too," added Rosie.

Vet Julie and Ansley's mom talked for a few more minutes while the girls continue to hug Lucky and tell him they will be coming back soon to take him home. They all hug Lucky one last time and went outside and hopped into the truck. Time to head to the town park for a fun filled afternoon of games followed by a picnic.

As soon as the truck stopped, Ansley jumped out saying, "Come on Rosie, let's sign up for the horseshoe toss and the volleyball tournament."

"OK sounds fun," replied Rosie.

After the games were finished, they all settled down to eat their hot dogs, fries and some watermelon.

Just as they were cleaning up, the mayor shouted, "It's starting to get late so grab your jars and head out to the big open field."

Everyone found a spot where they thought they would catch the most lightning bugs. Just as the sun dipped out of sight, the mayor rang the bell to start the contest.

Rosie started running around in circles chasing after bugs.

"Wow, this is hard," she called to Ansley.

"No, it isn't," answered Ansley, "Slow down for a minute and watch."

Ansley immediately caught one, then another and another. Rosie tried doing what Ansley was doing and was able to catch three.

The mayor rang the bell and called, "Alright, the contest is over. Count your bugs."

After everyone reported their numbers, the mayor declared, "The winner is the scout troop leader John."

Just then Rosie nudged Ansley and says, "Look, there is that boy scout that was out at the farm the other day that we were fishing with. Remember?"

"Yes, I remember him," replied Ansley while she was trying not to look at him because if she had caught two more lightning bugs, she would have been the winner.

Before Ansley could actually say anything, her mom patted her on the shoulder and said, "Come on girls, it's late. Let's go home."

They gathered up all their things, piled into the truck, and started home.

"That was fun," exclaimed Rosie. "I suck at catching lightning bugs, but I really did have fun trying."

Both of the girls were tired and were having trouble staying awake.

As they were dragging up the steps of the porch, they could hear the phone ringing. They went running up the rest of the steps and through the door just as Toots was picking up the phone.

"Oh, hello, how's it going? Yes, right, we went to the town picnic. I'm glad you called back. So, there is nothing new to report. Yes, I'll let her know. Thanks again for calling back. Be careful and we miss you." Toots hung up the phone and turned to Rosie saying, "That was your Uncle Don. He says they haven't found your parents yet, but there is still hope and they are still looking."

"Ok," Rosie sadly replied and then she added, "I'm going to go on up to take a shower."

After Rosie was out of sight, Ansley asked her mom, "What are you not telling Rosie?"

Her mom thought for a minute before saying, "Well Ansley, they have found some more people. Some were alive, but some were dead. Your dad assured me that there is still hope. So, we will tell Rosie the good news. We will hold back the bad news and hope we never have to say it about your aunt and uncle."

"I think that's a good idea," replied Ansley. "I know Dad will find them. He's the best."

"I'm sure he will," agreed Ansley's mom. "Now it's time for bed and don't you girls stay up too late. Good night, Ansley."

Ansley went up the stairs and hopped in the shower. By the time she finished and climbed in her bed, Rosie was already drifting off to sleep.

Ansley lay there thinking for a minute before saying, "Good night Rosie. Get a good night's sleep because tomorrow we are going treasure hunting."

"Ok, good night," sleepily agreed Rosie.

Chapter 11

"What in the world? That rooster is on the roof!" exclaimed Ansley jumping out of the bed. She looked out the window saying, "Cock-a-doodle-do to you too, now get off of that roof."

Rosie looked out the window also and asked, "How did he get up on the roof?"

Ansley replied, "He flies up into the tree and then over onto the roof. Hey, come on, let's get dressed, eat breakfast, pack a lunch and hit the river."

It only took a few minutes for them to get dressed and go running down the steps. They gobbled down their breakfast, packed a lunch, filled up their water bottles and started out the door.

Toots called out, "Hey girls, are you forgetting something?"

"What?" asked Rosie.

"Huh hum, the barn chores," replied Ansley's mom.

"Oh, Mom, would you please, pretty please, do the barn chores today?" pleaded Ansley.

Toots chuckled, "I already did them, you sleepy heads."

Both girls ran and hugged her crying, "Thanks, you're the best."

They grabbed their lunches and water bottles and went running outside and down the steps. It only took a few minutes to untie their kayaks and get them into the river.

"Wow," exclaimed Rosie. "The water is so clear and clean and calm.

It's hard to believe this is the same river that was raging last week."

"It sure is," replied Ansley as they started paddling across the river toward the island. "Just look at all that trash and debris, we should definitely find some treasure today."

"Like what?" asked Rosie.

The girls found a good clear spot to hop out and pull their kayaks onto the island.

Immediately, Ansley bent down and said to Rosie, "Look at this really cool old bottle I just found."

At almost the same time, Rosie said, "Hey Ansley, look, there is a hole over there in the river bank."

Ansley just shrugged it off saying, "That old hole has been there as long as I've been coming here."

The girls started walking around the island finding some coins, several more bottles, and a lawn chair.

All at once Ansley grabbed Rosie's arm and said, "Look, there's a canoe, let's check it out."

Both girls start pulling the trash and broken tree branches off of the canoe. When they finally were able to pull the canoe out, a tree swayed and they heard a funny squeaky noise.

Ansley jumped back a little and said, "Look, there's that big fish tail."

Rosie looked and replied, "I think that's a swimmer's board with a fish tail decal."

The girls moved some more branches and debris and saw that it actually was a fish tail and it was attached to a body.

"Oh my," exclaimed Ansley, "What is this?" and then she said, "Come on Rosie, give me a hand. This thing is huge."

The girls finished uncovering the rest of the fish tail and rolled it over. Then they jumped back clutching on to each other in excitement and a little fearful at first. They had just found the often-fantasized Greenbrier River mermaid. They had heard different stories from people saying that a mermaid lived in the river but no one had ever been able to get a picture.

Rosie was still kind of scared and opened her mouth to scream. Ansley was able to put her hand over Rosie's mouth before any sound could come out.

She calmly told Rosie, "Shuuuuu, shuu, if you scream, Mom will come to check on us."

She looked at Rosie to make sure she was in agreement and took her hand off her mouth.

Rosie looked down and asked Ansley, "Is it real, is it breathing?"

Ansley knew what to do from her experience working with the farm animals with her dad. She reached for the mermaid's arm and checked for a pulse.

Ansley looked up at Rosie with wonder in her eyes saying. "I feel a pulse."

Rosie replied with, "Are you kidding me? That's a mermaid."

Ansley jumped up dancing around saying, "It's alive and yes, it looks that way."

"But, but, but how? Oh, my how did it get here?" asked Rosie.

Ansley thought for a minute and replied, "Well, we have been having storms in the oceans and the oceans connect to the rivers and here we are on the river."

Rosie is still a little shook up and stuttered, "Yes, but it's a mermaid. What if she wakes up and bites us?"

Ansley was too excited to think about that possibility. She was worried about the mermaid. She was halfway talking to herself saying, "First we have to check her out. Look, her right arm is cut and bleeding. It definitely needs a dressing."

"Well," replied Rosie, "I think we should get some duct tape and tape her mouth shut."

Ansley was starting to get impatient, "Rosie, she is knocked out. She can't bite."

Rosie still wasn't convinced and replied, "She'll wake up."

Ansley knew the mermaid was badly hurt and answered, "Maybe."

Ansley checked the mermaid's pulse again and turned to Rosie and very seriously said, "I'm going to tell you where the first aid is. I want you to hurry up and go get it. Try not to let Mom see you. I'm afraid she would call the authorities and they would come and get her."

"Ok," answered Rosie. "But what if she sees me getting the kit? What should I say?"

Ansley thought for a minute and finally said, "Tell her I cut my finger. It's not bad, but it's bleeding and I want to clean it and put on a bandage so it won't get infected."

"Ok," replied Rosie as she jumped in her kayak and started back across the river.

Ansley finished getting the rest of the sticks and rubbish off of the mermaid. Then she got her water bottle and took off her outer shirt. She wet the shirt and wiped off the mermaid's face and arms very gently. Then she noticed the swim top that the mermaid had on. It was her lost top that blew off the clothes line last spring.

In the meantime, Rosie was able to get across the river, find the first aid kit, and was getting in her kayak to start back across the river just as Ansley's mom turned the corner coming back from the barn.

Out of the corner of her eye, she saw Rosie and called, "Hey Rosie, is everything alright?"

She climbed on into the kayak and responded, "Yes, Aunt Toots, everything is ok. I just needed to grab something for Ansley."

She paddled as fast as she could and reached the island out of breath and in record time. She jumped out, grabbed the kit and went running to Ansley who was knelling down beside the mermaid.

Ansley looked up and said, "I heard Mom calling to you. Did you tell her?"

"I just told her I needed to grab something for you," replied Rosie.

Ansley sighed with relief, "That's good. Now help me finish cleaning her arm so I can get it bandaged."

They finished cleaning her up, bandaged her arm, and then they gently leaned her up against the tree.

"Wow," exclaimed Rosie, "It really is a mermaid. I still can't believe it."

"Yes, it really is a mermaid," replied Ansley, "And we can't tell anyone. I mean anyone!"

"What do we do now?" asked Rosie.

Ansley replied, "I've done everything I know how to do. Now we just wait and see if she wakes up."

They sat there for several hours just watching her breathe. The sun was getting pretty low in the sky when they heard the dinner bell ringing.

Ansley thought for a minute and then told Rosie, "Go to the other side of the island and tell Mom that we are still finding treasure and we will be home soon."

Rosie ran to the edge of the island and saw her Aunt Toots was getting ready to ring the bell again.

She yelled, "We'll be home before dark."

"Ok," answered Ansley's mom. "Don't take too long, dinner will be ready soon."

Rosie went running back to Ansley and panted, "Dinner will be ready soon. What are we going to do now?"

Ansley hesitated before replying, "Well, she still isn't awake and there's a big knot on the back of her head. Let's go home and eat and I guess we'll have to slip back over later."

"What if she wakes up while we are gone?" wondered Rosie.

Ansley replied, "Come on, I tied her waist to that tree with a piece of rope I had in my kayak. It just so happens that the boy scout taught me how to tie some good knots the day we were fishing so she won't be able to get loose."

"Ok, if you say so," answered Rosie, "I'm starved."

"Me too, now that you mention it," replied Ansley.

Both girls took off running and jumped into their kayaks. Within a matter of minutes, they paddled across the river, tied up their kayaks, ran up the steps, and washed up. They were sitting down at the table when Ansley's mom set down a big bowl of spaghetti in the middle of the table. Before Toots could even sit down both girls had served themselves and was starting to eat.

"Hey Mom, this spaghetti is really delicious," said Ansley in between mouthfuls.

"Really?" answered her mom. "I'm surprised you can even taste it you are eating so fast."

"I'm really hungry Mom," answered Ansley. "You can really work up an appetite hunting treasure."

Rosie chimed in, "For sure, hunting treasure makes you hungry."

The girls finished gobbling up their dinner, jumped up to help clear the table and wash the dishes.

They were starting out the door when they heard Ansley's mom saying, "Wait. Take this leftover corn out to the chickens."

Ansley was halfway down the steps and wanted to get back to the mermaid.

She questioned her mom, "Now? Can we do it later?"

Her mom replied, "Now, and gather the eggs while you are out there."

Ansley remembered that she was supposed to be helping her mom more while her dad was away so she grabbed the egg basket and said, "Come on Rosie, let's go."

Both girls went flying down the steps and ran to the barn.

Ansley said, "Rosie, I'll get the eggs if you will throw the corn to the chickens."

"Ok," replied Rosie.

Before Rosie could throw the corn, Ansley yelled, "Come here, I've got something to show you."

"What is it?" answered Rosie.

"Come on and see," teased Ansley.

"What are you looking at?" asked Rosie. "Oh my gosh," screamed Rosie, "It's a snake."

"Don't be scared, it's just Henry the blacksnake, He won't hurt you," calmly responded Ansley.

"You got that right," Rosie replied in a semi-shout. "I'm not getting near him!"

"You chicken," giggled Ansley.

"Yep," replied Rosie just as Ansley picked up Henry and started chasing Rosie around the barn.

Rosie is running and screaming, "Stop, STOP."

"He won't hurt you," laughed Ansley.

Rosie picked up an egg out of the egg basket and threw it at Ansley. It was a lucky shot and it hit her in the head. The egg cracked open and it went running down her face.

Ansley stopped chasing Rosie and said, "You asked for it, you're going to get it now."

She put Henry the snake down, picked up an egg, threw it at Rosie, hitting her in the arm.

"Well, watch this," yelled Rosie as she was turning on the water hose. She turned it on full blast and sprayed Ansley.

Ansley turned around and picked up another egg to throw.

Before she could aim it at Rosie, she heard her mom calling, "What are you girls doing? Get those eggs up here to the house right NOW."

"Ok Mom," replied Ansley.

Both girls started laughing and quickly cleaned the egg off of themselves.

Ansley picked up the egg basket and they walked back to the house.

"Here you go Mom, here's the eggs," announced Ansley.

"We didn't get many this evening, did we?" questioned Ansley's mom.

"Well, a few got busted," replied Ansley.

"Yep," chimed in Rosie.

Then Ansley's mom asked, "And why are you girls wet?"

"We were hot so we sprayed ourselves with the water hose," replied Ansley.

"Yes, we were hot," added Rosie.

"Well, take your hot selves with your egg arm and faces to the shower," replied Toots.

"Ok, we will," responded Rosie without any objection.

The girls went up the stairs without saying anything to take their showers.

When they came back downstairs, they quickly gathered up some cans of tuna fish, crackers, apples, bananas and put it all into a bag.

"Mom," called Ansley, "We are going over to the island for a little while."

"Ok, but be back by dark," answered her mom.

"Thanks Mom, we will," replied Ansley.

The girls grabbed the bag of food and their water bottles and untied their kayaks. They jumped in and head across the river toward the island.

Chapter 12

"Hurry up Rosie, paddle faster," urged Ansley as they were getting closer to the island.

"I am," replied Rosie. The girls grabbed the bag of food and their water bottles.

They ran to the spot where they had left the mermaid. They quickly looked around and couldn't find the mermaid anywhere.

"That's great," Rosie exclaimed, "You didn't tie her up very good."

"I most certainly did," replied Ansley.

"Well, where is she?" questioned Rosie.

"Like I'm supposed to know?" replied Ansley. "Let's see if we can find her."

The girls start looking around. They look from one end of the island to the other.

Just as they were starting to lose hope Rosie bent down and said, "Hey Ansley, look at this skid mark, it looks like she went into the water here."

They look around and saw an old dead tree that had fallen and revealed a hole in the river bank.

"Mmmm, I've never seen that hole before," murmured Ansley.

"Probably because that tree must have fallen during the flood and that hole was hidden by that big old tree," replied Rosie. "I'll bet she's in there."

The water on this part of the river is shallow so the girls just took off running. They quickly reached the hole and realized it was a small cave.

They called out, "Hello, is anyone in there."

All they heard was an echo.

"Now what?" asked Rosie.

"We will go back to the house and get a rope and a lantern," answered Ansley.

"For what?" asked Rosie.

"Well, we'll need the lantern so we can see and the rope in case we have to climb down into that cave," replied Ansley.

The girls run back around the island, climbed into their kayaks and paddled back to the house. They ran to the house and grabbed a lantern. Then they ran to the shed and grabbed a rope.

They were running down the path to the river when Toots came out onto the porch calling, "Come on in girls, it's time for dinner."

"We're not hungry, Mom," Ansley called back.

"Well, you aren't going back across the river. It's too late. Now you girls get inside and wash up for dinner."

"Ok, Mom," replied Ansley.

"Now what?" asked Rosie.

"Well, let's put the rope and the lantern by this tree and first thing in the morning we'll   check out that cave," whispered Ansley.

"You mean after we do the barn chores," replied Rosie.

"No," Ansley responded. "We are getting up early before Mom wakes up and heading across the river."

"Girls, come on, before dinner gets cold," Toots called for them again.

"Oh boy, hot dogs and for dessert strawberry shortcake. Yum," cheered Rosie as she was rubbing her belly.

As they were sitting down at the table Ansley asked her mom, "Did Vet Julie call?"

"As a matter of fact, she did," replied her mom. "She said we can come visit Lucky Dog tomorrow afternoon."

"Wow, that's awesome," cried Ansley.

Rosie exclaimed, "Man, these hot dogs are really good Aunt Toots."

"Thanks Rosie, they are all-beef," responded Toots.

"Pass the French fries and ketchup please," Ansley was really hungry after all.

The girls quickly finished eating, helped clean up the dinner dishes, and went upstairs to shower. They put on their sleeping clothes and went back downstairs to watch a movie and eat a dish of that strawberry short-cake.

"Hey Mom, what movie are we watching tonight?" asked Ansley.

Her mom replied, "It's called *Splash*. It's an older one but I think you will like it. It stars Tom Hanks and Daryl Hannah. It's about a mermaid."

Ansley replied excitedly, "That really sounds like it will be fun."

Rosie leaned over and whispered, "Do you think she knows?"

"Do you think I know what?" inquired Toots.

"Oh, how did you know that this is Rosie's favorite movie and she's watched it a hundred times," quickly replied Ansley.

"Yes, that's right," chimed in Rosie, "And tonight will make one hundred and one."

"Alright girls, let's get our cake and add the whipped cream. Get our milk and settle down to watch the movie," urged Ansley's mom.

As soon as the movie was over, they all head to bed.

After they get snuggled into bed, Rosie asked Ansley, "Do you really think we'll find her?"

Ansley immediately replied, "Yep, because her arm is really hurt bad and I think she knows we want to help her."

Chapter 13

"Rosie, Rosie, wake up, get up," insisted Ansley as she was shaking Rosie.

"What, what is it?" mumbled Rosie as she rolled over.

"It's daylight, come on let's go," urged Ansley.

Rosie exclaimed, "Really, what time is it anyway?"

"I don't know, probably 5:30 or 6:00. I'm not sure," replied Ansley.

"Are you kidding me?" mumbled Rosie rolling back over. "I'm going back to sleep."

Ansley bent over and whispered in her ear, "The mermaid".

Rosie's eyes opened wide and she quickly climbed out of bed.

The girls quietly dressed and walked softly down the stairs.

Ansley whispered, "Rosie, get a granola bar, a banana, and a bottle of water for both of us. I'll grab our water shoes."

"Ok, I will" ," replies Rosie.

They slipped out onto the porch and quickly put on their water shoes. They went down the twelve porch steps without a sound and went running to their kayaks.

Ansley stopped abruptly and told Rosie, "Wait a minute."

She went running back to get the lantern and rope where she had stashed them the evening before. She quickly grabbed them, went running back, and stowed them in her kayak. Both girls shoved their kayaks into the river and quickly paddled across the river to the hole. They jumped out, pulled their kayaks onto the bank and grabbed their supplies.

"Ok, I'll tie this end of the rope around this tree to secure it and go in the hole," declared Ansley as she was tying the other end of the rope around her waist.

"Wait a minute," cautioned Rosie. "Suppose it goes straight down?"

"Then I'll rappel," countered Ansley.

"Do you know how to do that?" asked Rosie.

Ansley quickly answered, "Yes Rosie. Dad taught me. You have to be able to climb and rappel to be a rescue swimmer."

"Ok, be careful," added Rosie. "Here's the lantern."

Ansley searched in her supplies bag and brought out some sticks and handed a few to Rosie saying, "Here, bend these light sticks until they light up."

They bent the light sticks and toss them into the hole and looked in.

"Wow, it is a small cave," chattered Rosie.

"Good," replied Ansley. "Let's hope it's a small cave with no other exits."

Ansley made sure the rope was still secure and sat down at the edge of the hole. She went scooting down the incline for about four feet until her feet hit level ground. She held up the lantern and looked around at the small rocks and dripping water.

"Are you ok? What do you see down there?" shouted Rosie.

"The usual so far," replied Ansley as she took a few steps to her right.

She felt something under her foot and bent down for a closer look. She picked up the object , brushed it off and realized it was a bracelet.

"Hey Rosie, I found a bracelet and WOW it looks like it is covered in diamonds," shouted Ansley.

Rosie quickly grabbed another rope and tied one end to her waist and the other end to the tree. She got her flashlight, ran over to the hole, sat down and went sliding down into the cave. Her feet hit the bottom and she jumped up. Both girls looked at the bracelet. Then they looked around and realized that they were in a big, dark space with water dripping down the walls.

"This is a big room," declared Ansley. "But where is the mermaid?"

They started yelling but all they heard were their echoes.

Rosie was starting to get impatient and asked, "So Ansley, where is she?"

Ansley was getting a little worried and snapped, "Like I know."

The girls continued looking around behind the rocks and suddenly Ansley exclaimed, "Look at this pile of rings and necklaces."

Rosie was exploring behind another rock and squealed, "Hey, come look at this; it's a wallet, a dry bag, sun screen, some towels and wow, a cell phone." She picked up the cell phone and said, "Let's call the house and see if it works."

Ansley grabbed the phone and cautioned Rosie, "Are you crazy? You'll wake up Mom."

"I guess you're right, not a good idea," replied Rosie.

Then the girls see a large rock formation and shine their lights so they could see what was on the other side. They saw two eyes shining in the darkness. They screamed and jumped back in surprise.

Ansley quickly recovered and exclaimed, "She's awake."

"No crap, those eyes scared me at first," replied Rosie.

Ansley quickly scurried around the rocks and there lay the mermaid in a pool of water. She was looking up, holding her right arm up and not moving.

Rosie made it around the rocks and looked at the mermaid, then Ansley and all she could say was, "Wow, a real mermaid."

Ansley bent over to get a better look at her arm and murmured, "Look at her arm, it's infected."

"I wonder if she can talk, she's half human," wondered Rosie out loud.

"I guess you should ask her," replied Ansley.

Rosie leaned over and said, "hi" to the mermaid and the mermaid just looked at them.

Then Ansley asked her, "Do you have a name?"

Again, there was no response.

"Do you think she'll let us clean her arm now that she's awake?" questioned Rosie.

"We can try," answered Ansley.

Ansley took off her backpack and took out the first aid kit and two small candles.

"What're the candles for?" asked Rosie, "We've got the lantern and flashlights."

"You'll see," replied Ansley.

She slowly inched closer to the mermaid and reached out her hand. The mermaid just kept starring at her but didn't move. Then she leaned over and touched the mermaid's right hand and the mermaid pulled her hand back. Then Ansley touched her left hand and she didn't pull it back. She slowly took hold of the mermaids left hand and gently held it. The mermaid slowly closed and opened her eyes and just laid there.

Ansley tells the mermaid , "It's ok, we won't hurt you. But if we don't clean your right arm you are going to get very sick."

Ansley let go of the mermaid's hand and opened the first aid kit. To demonstrate she put some alcohol on her own right arm, flinched a little and then wiped it with a gauze pad. Then she wrapped her arm with an ace bandage. Ansley then leaned down and poured some clean water on the mermaid's arm. The mermaid didn't move so she poured some hydro peroxide on the mermaid's arm. So far so good so she gently applied some anti-bacterial cream, then a non-stick pad. Finally, she wrapped the mermaid's arm with an ace bandage.

Ansley stood up and looked at Rosie and slowly said, "Her arm looks bad, it's all red and infected."

She sat down and patted the rock next to her indicating for Rosie to sit down also. She picked up the two candles and lite them and handed one to Rosie. Then she started singing "This Little Light of Mine" and Rosie joined in.

They sat there singing, *"This Little Light of Mine, I'm going to let it shine. This Little Light of Mine, I'm going to let it shine. This Little Light of Mine, I'm going to let it shine. Let it shine, all the time, let it shine."*

When they finished the song, Rosie asked, "Why are we singing?"

Ansley replied, "Well, when my granny was alive, she would take me with her when she went to visit people that was hurt or sick. She would always take cookies and candles and then she would sing. She had a beautiful voice and the people always said that they felt better so I asked her one time about it. She told me 'we all are like lights and sometimes our lights get dim so if we get together with our lights with someone who has a dim light and sing and pray it helps them to heal. The more lights, the more healing.' She also said 'Ansley, let your little light shine. If everyone would shine and smile and be kind, we would have a better world. Don't you ever forget that Ansley.'"

"Wow," exclaimed Rosie as tears rolled down her face. Then she said, "Ansley, can we sing that again with our candles lit and so loud that the rescue workers that are looking for Mom and Dad can hear it."

Without saying anything, they both started singing together in their loudest voice and it echoed back again and again. *"This Little Light of Mine, I'm going to let it shine. This Little Light of Mine, I'm going to let it shine. This Little Light of Mine, I'm going to let it shine. Let it shine, all the time, let it shine."* When they finished, they just stood there looking at the mermaid.

Rosie gently nudges Ansley and whispered, "Look, she's asleep."

"Yes," replied Ansley, "but her arm doesn't look so good."

Rosie thought for a minute and finally said, Yyou know you are right. We all have lights and talents; we might not have the talent to fix her arm but I bet Vet Julie does."

"No, we can't tell anyone. If we let anyone else know someone will eventually come and trap her and take her away for experiments or maybe something even worse," declared Ansley.

"We aren't going to tell anyone but Vet Julie," argued Rosie. Then she added, "If we don't and her arm gets worse, she could die."

Ansley finally looked at Rosie and agreed, "you are right. We need to get Vet Julie to look at it."

They were trying to figure out how to get that done when they heard the porch bell.

Chapter 14

The girls run back to their kayaks, climb in, and paddled back across the river. They drag their kayaks onto the bank and tie them up.

Ansley's mom was on the porch and called, "Have you girls done the barn chores yet?"

"No," they both replied.

"Then hurry up and get them done. Breakfast is almost ready," shouts Toots

They took off to the barn planning all the way about dividing up the chores and about the mermaid.

They quickly got the animals fed and watered and then headed back to the house.

Ansley's mom was waiting for them full of questions. "What have you girls been up to this morning? We have to get those eggs gathered the first thing in the mornings. What were you doing across the river?"

Ansley quickly replied, "Treasure hunting."

"Yes, treasure hunting," added Rosie.

"Well girls that's ok, just remember chores are to be done before treasure hunting. Is that clear?" stated Ansley's mom.

"Yes ma'am," both girls immediately replied.

"Now wash up and eat your breakfast. Vet Julie called and wants us at her office," added Ansley's mom.

"Ok," replied Ansley.

The girls wash up and quickly eat breakfast. As soon as they finish, they all got into the truck and headed into town.

"Mom?" asked Ansley, "What's up?"

Her mom answered, "Well Ansley, Lucky Dog is doing well, except his left leg."

"What do you mean?" asked Ansley.

Her mom replied, "Lucky has gangrene in his leg."

"What's that?" questioned Ansley.

Her mom told her, "It's a very bad infection."

"So, Vet Julie and her nurses are going to give him some medicine, right?" replied Ansley.

"They have been giving him some different medicines but they aren't working," answered her mom.

"So, what are they going to do now?" asked Rosie.

"We'll see what Vet Julie thinks," said Ansley's mom as they pulled into the parking lot.

They jumped out of the truck and as they went running in, they could see Lucky Dog laying on the operating table.

"What's wrong? What are you doing?" yelled Ansley.

"Ansley," said Vet Julie, "I'm going to have to take Lucky Dog's left leg off."

"No, no," cried Ansley.

"Ansley, if I don't amputate his leg, he isn't going to make it. The infection is spreading and the medicine isn't stopping it," replied Vet Julie.

Ansley fell across the table and Lucky Dog crying uncontrollably.

Vet Julie put her hand on Ansley's back and leaned over petting Lucky Dog. She softly said, "Ansley, if we take the leg off, he will live. He will learn how to walk on three legs if we help him and he'll be alive. If we leave the leg on, he will die."

"Ok," sobs Ansley as she hugs Lucky Dog and whispers in his ear, "You are a great dog and buddy. We can do this."

"Ok then," Vet Julie said as she turned to Ansley's mom, "You'll need to sign this medical release form."

"Alright, we are depending on you," replied Ansley's mom.

Vet Julie told them all to please go to the waiting room and she would let them know when she was finished. They left the room and turned for one last look as the door shut behind them.

As they were sitting in the waiting room Ansley asked, "Hey Mom, do you have a candle?"

She answered, "No, but I have a lighter, why?"

"Well, remember Granny and what she did for people and how she sang 'This Little Light of Mine'?"

"I do remember," answered her mom.

"Well," said Ansley, "Please get out your lighter and we'll sing it."

Toots quickly got out her lighter and they sang "This Little Light of Mine I'm going to let it Shine". They sang it several times as they sat there waiting. They prayed and then they sat there in silence.

After what seemed like hours, Vet Julie came into the waiting room and announced, "Lucky Dog pulled through and now we wait. He's resting now. You all can go home now. I'll call you later and you can come back tomorrow."

The girls jumped up and hugged Vet Julie.

Ansley's mom said, "Thank you, we'll see you tomorrow."

They were quiet on the ride home.

When they parked the truck, Ansley's mom said, "Girls, I'll fix some sandwiches for lunch. They will be ready in a few minutes and we'll eat by the river. Sound Good?"

"Yell for us," the girls reply and, "Can we go treasure hunting for a little bit?"

Toots thought for a minute and replied, "Ok, I'll ring the bell when I have lunch fixed."

The girls race off to the river and untie their kayaks. They jumped in and quickly paddle across to the island. They drag the kayaks up on shore and run to the hole where they last seen the mermaid. They sit down at the edge and slide down in. Ansley grabbed the lantern and looked around. To their surprise, the mermaid was awake and sitting next to the wall of the cave. Her tail from the waist down was in the water and she was holding her arm up against her chest. Ansley opened up the food bag and laid out a towel. Then she laid out an apple, a cookie, some chips, and peanuts. The mermaid slowly leaned over and pickup up the apple and took a big bite.

"Wow," whispered Rosie, "She's eating."

Then Ansley took out two bottles of water and took a drink from hers. The mermaid leaned over and took a drink from the river water.

"Well, she's eating and drinking. That's a good sign," said Ansley.

"Yes, that's good, but look at her arm. It's all red and it has yellow stuff leaking out of it," pointed out Rosie.

"Yes, I see that. I think I need to put on some more antibiotic cream and redress it. Hand me the supplies Rosie," answered Ansley.

Ansley slowly leaned over and touched the mermaid's hand. The mermaid raised her arm to let Ansley clean it, put on the medication and rewrap it.

"There, all done, you are very brave and you did great," Ansley softly told the mermaid.

The mermaid just looked at the girls with her big, beautiful eyes.

"Ansley, that arm is really infected and if we don't get Vet Julie to doctor it, she'll die," Rosie said in a scared voice.

"I know," replied Ansley. "I'm still not sure we can trust Vet Julie."

"I think we are going to have to," was all Rosie could say.

They sat down and smile at the mermaid trying to figure out what to do and she just stared back at them.

Ansley finally said, "I'll bet lunch is ready so we had better head back."

The girls slowly stood up and waved bye to the mermaid and her eyes followed them as they climbed out of the cave.

They paddled back across the river and as they were tying up their kayaks, they heard Ansley's mom calling, "Lunch is ready. Wash up girls."

"We will," they both answered at the same time.

They quickly washed their hands and sat down at the table.

Ansley looked at her lunch and asked, "Mom, what is this?"

"Tuna fish, why?" answered her mom.

"Oh, no actual reason. Just asking," replied Ansley.

The girls hurriedly ate their lunch, cleared their dishes and headed toward the door.

Ansley's mom stopped them saying, "Hold up girls, I need you to go up the river trail and pick some blackberries."

"Now, Mom? Can we do it later?" asked Ansley.

"Yes, right now. Go get the buckets and rope," answered her mom.

Ansley went to the hall closet and got the buckets and rope.

Rosie was a little puzzled and asked, "What's the rope for?"

Ansley answered, "We can put a piece of the rope through the handle of the bucket and then tie it around our waist."

Rosie was still puzzled and asked, "Why?"

Ansley replied, "That way you have both hands free to pick and we can get done faster."

"Ok. I get it," said Rosie.

"Good," agreed Ansley, "because we need to pick as fast as we can."

The girls were starting out the door when Ansley's mom stopped them. She gave each of them a water bottle and a snack bag. Then she told them, "Pick enough for two pies and watch for snakes."

"Snakes!" shouts Rosie.

"Yep snakes, your favorite," giggled Ansley, "They like blackberries and toes."

"Are you kidding me?" questioned Rosie.

"Nope, it's true," answered Ansley.

"She's right," added Ansley's mom. "Wear hiking shoes."

The girls grab the water bottles, snack bags, ropes, and buckets and take off down the steps. Ansley showed Rosie how to put her snack bag and water bottle in the bucket. Then she tied the bucket to the handle bars with the piece of rope.

She turned to Rosie and asked, "Got it."
Rosie gave her the thumbs up and answered, "Yes."

Chapter 15

The girls started down the river trail and Rosie asked, "Do cars come on the trail?"

"Nope," answered Ansley.

Rosie asked, "Why not?"

"Because this used to be a train track trail. The train doesn't run anymore so they took up the tracks and now no motor vehicles. Only walkers, bikes and horses are allowed," answered Ansley.

"Well, I saw a pickup truck the other morning," argued Rosie.

"Oh, that was the park ranger," replied Ansley. "They are allowed because they have to check to make sure no fallen trees, or rocks have rolled on to the trail."

As they ride along the river is on their left and the hillside is to the right. The air was cool due to the trees and hillside shading most of the trail.

Just then Ansley pointed and said, "Look Rosie, a blue heron."

Rosie looked and said, "Wow, look how elegant it is when it flies."

Ansley said, "This looks like a good patch, let's stop here."

The girls got off of their bikes, tied the ropes with the buckets around their waists, and started picking berries.

"Let's hurry," Ansley urged Rosie. "We need to check on the mermaid."

"I'm trying but I keep on squishing mine," replied Rosie.

"Look," replied Ansley. "Pull from the top of the berry and it will roll into your hand like this," coached Ansley. Ansley watched as Rosie tried. "Holy cow Rosie, have you never picked berries before?" asked Ansley.

"Not really, unless you count picking them up in the store," answered Rosie.

"Are you kidding me?" asked Ansley.

"Well Ansley, everyone doesn't live in the country like you do," countered Rosie.

"I guess that's true," returned Ansley. "I'm glad I do."

"I wish I did," sighed Rosie.

"Oh well, for now you do so let's hurry and get our buckets full so we can head back," responded Ansley.

The girls pick in silence for a while and in the meantime the sun has peeped up over the mountain and it has gotten hotter. The bugs have started biting and the girls are trying to pick berries with one hand and are swatting bugs with the other hand.

"Hey Ansley," said Rosie, "It looks like our buckets are full. This isn't fun anymore so can we go?"

"Sounds good to me," replied Ansley.

Rosie turned around to get out of the bushes, saw a snake, tripped over a rock, and berries went flying everywhere.

She jumped back up and Ansley asked, "What's up?"

Rosie shakenly replied, "It's a snake."

Ansley looked and saw a big long black snake lazing in the sun and said, "He won't hurt you. It's just a black snake and they like berries."

"Well, like I know that," fumed Rosie.

"We call him Henry," commented Ansley.

"Are all snakes Henry?" asked Rosie.

"Yes," replied Ansley.

"Well Henry made me spill my berries," retorted Rosie. "What are we going to do now?"

"Don't worry," replied Ansley. "Not a problem, here we'll pick up what we can and I'll give you some of mine."

When they had picked up what they could Ansley took the two buckets and put the same number of berries in both.

"Now, that will be plenty for two pies. Let's head back," she said to Rosie.

"Wait a minute," Rosie requested. "I'm thirsty and hungry."

They sat down on the edge of the trail in the shade and look down at the river. They watch the water flow by and look up at the blue sky and the white clouds drifting by.

"Look at that cloud, it looks like a lion," whispered Ansley.

"What? A lion? Where?" Rosie cried.

"There in the sky. That cloud looks like a lion, you silly thing," laughed Ansley.

"That wasn't funny," muttered Rosie.

"Rosie, if you lay back and look at the clouds and use your imagination you can see all kinds of things in the clouds. Look over there: it's a duck." Pointed out Ansley.

"Oh, that looks like a pig," chimed in Rosie.

"Now you got it," laughed Ansley.

The girls were lying there pointing out what they were seeing when a horseman came around the curve and shouted, "You girls ok?"

"Yes, we're just cloud watching," laughed Ansley.

The horseman laughed, tipped his hat, trotted around them, and continued on up the trail. The girls remembered they needed to check on the mermaid so they jumped up and quickly gathered up their things. They hopped on their bikes and headed home. They peddled at a steady pace and arrived home in record time. They parked their bikes and took the berries into the house.

Toots looked at the buckets and said, "I thought your buckets would be full as long as you girls have been gone."

Ansley explained, "Mom, Rosie saw a snake, tripped over a rock, and spilled hers."

"Are you ok?" asked Ansley's mom.

"Yes, I'm sorry I spilled my bucket," replied Rosie.

"That's ok, I'm just glad you didn't get hurt. I'm sure there is still enough berries for one pie and maybe two. Thank you, girls," said Ansley's mom as she gave them a hug.

They were interrupted when the phone started ringing.

Ansley was closest so she answered, "Hello, Dad, is that you? Is everything ok? Yes, we are all doing well. Rosie and I went berry picking and just got home. Yes, she's here. Mom, it's Dad."

Ansley handed the phone to her mom and Toots said, "Hello Don, how are you? How are things going with the search? Really, that's great news. Yes, Rosie is here right beside me. Oh, Lucky Dog is doing better but they did have to amputate his left leg. Rosie, your Uncle Don wants to talk to you," and she handed the phone to Rosie.

Rosie grabbed the phone and hastily said, "Hi, Uncle Don, what's happening?"

He replied, "Rosie, we found another survivor that had drifted up on an island so there is still hope for your parents. We know that all of the people that got off the yacht did have their life jackets on. So stay positive because we are still searching."

"Ok thank you Uncle Don and you be safe. We love you. Here's Aunt Toots," Rosie turned around and handed the phone back to Aunt Toots and said, "Uncle Don wants to talk to you again."

The girls went outside and ran down to the river. They jumped into their kayaks and quickly paddled over to the island.

As they were tying up their kayaks, Ansley said, "Rosie, my dad will find your parents. After all it is his brother that he's looking for and he won't give up."

"I know," replied Rosie. "This waiting and not knowing is just so hard."

They quickly ran to the cave and scrambled in. They found the mermaid awake and drinking water, but noticed that her arm still looked infected. They sat and sang to the mermaid and didn't even realize that they were actually feeling better.

Suddenly Ansley said, "Look, she seems to like it. Hello, can you talk?"

No answer. Ansley waved her left hand back and forth. The mermaid waved her left hand back and forth.

"Wow," exclaimed Rosie, "That's really neat."

Both girls wave their hands and say, "Hello."

The mermaid waved her hand and opened her mouth and out came a "ha" sound.

Ansley and Rosie looked at each other and waved their hands and say, "Hello, hello" over and over again.

Then Ansley said to Rosie, "Let's give her a break and see if she will eat something."

When they checked the bag of food they had left, it was empty. The mermaid had eaten it all.

"It looks like her appetite is good," chuckled Ansley.

"That's great," agreed Rosie. "So how about telling Vet Julie about her arm?"

"Ok," agreed Ansley. "We'll tell her tomorrow."

They paddled home in silence and went to bed early.

Chapter 16

" Wake up girls, time to get up. We can go check on Lucky this morning," called Ansley's mom.

The girls jumped out of bed, dressed and went running down the steps.

Ansley's mom said, "I'll get us breakfast at McDonald's," as she opened the door.

"That sounds good to me," cheered Ansley.

"Me too," added Rosie.

When they arrived at the vet's, Lucky Dog was laying down wagging his tail and when he saw them up popped his head. The girls looked at where his left leg used to be and remembered that it was no longer there.

"He'll be fine," said Vet Julie as she came into the room. "We have the infection and his pain under control. He is eating and drinking. I still want to keep him a little while longer to make sure that leg completely heals."

Ansley's mom said, "We got some good news from Don. They found another survivor and there is still hope for Rosie's parents."

"That's great news," replied Vet Julie.

"It sure is," added Rosie.

Suddenly, Toot's cell phone started ringing. She looked at the number and said, "Oh excuse me a minute, I have to answer this," and she walked into the other room.

Ansley, Rosie and Vet Julie are left alone with Lucky. Ansley looked around before asking, "Vet Julie, do you think you can come out to our place this evening for s'mores?"

"Well Ansley, it just so happens I'm going to be at my cabin up the river from your house. So yes, I can come over for some s'mores," she replied.

"That would be great," cheered Ansley. "How about 6 o'clock? Will that work for you?"

"Yes, 6 o'clock will work for me. I'll see you then," replied Vet Julie.

Ansley winked at Rosie and said, "Ok, we'll see you at the house around six."

Ansley's mom came back in and asked Ansley, "See who around six?"

Ansley answered, "Vet Julie, Mom. She's going to be at her camp this evening so I invited her by to roast hot dogs and make s'mores."

Ansley's mom smiled and said, "That was neighborly of you Ansley. We'll see you around six."

Vet Julie asked, "Can I bring anything?"

Ansley quickly said, "Chips would be great."

"I can do that," answered Vet Julie. "I'll see you all later."

All afternoon Ansley and Rosie had been trying to figure out how to tell Vet Julie about the mermaid or should they take her to the island treasure hunting. That evening when Vet Julie pulled into the driveway, she was driving her Vet truck which meant she would have some medical supplies. The girls ran down the steps to greet her as she was getting out of the truck.

"Hello," they shouted.

"Hi girls, here's some graham crackers and marshmallows for the campfire after dinner."

"Thank you," said Ansley. "Would you like to go treasure hunting with us?"

"Well, let's go see your mom and see if she needs any help getting everything ready for the campfire and dinner," answered Vet Julie.

They started up the steps when Toots came out the door to welcome Vet Julie, "I'm so glad you could make it."

"Thanks for inviting me," replied Vet Julie. "I needed a break."

"Well, it's a simple dinner so everyone wash your hands. We are making silver turtles," chuckled Ansley's mom.

"What's that?" questioned Vet Julie.

Ansley asked, "You've never heard of silver turtles?"

"No, what are they?" asked Vet Julie.

Ansley answered, "They are the best quick meal ever. You take a piece of aluminum foil and start with a piece of meat, a steak or even a hamburger patty. Then you add some cubed-up potatoes, diced carrots and onions. Add the spices you like and wrap it all up in the piece of foil. When you are finished it looks like a turtle shell. You can cook it in the oven, on the grill, or in the campfire."

Toots already had all the vegetables cut up. She handed everyone a piece of foil and said, "Ok, let's start making our turtles. Pick out what meat you want. Then add the number of potatoes, carrots and onions you want."

They joked about what their turtles would taste like and then put their turtles in the oven to cook. They cleaned up the leftovers and went out on the porch to relax and enjoy some lemonade.

Suddenly, Ansley said, "Hey, Vet Julie, we got an extra kayak out. Do you want to go treasure hunting? Mom, can we go for a little while?"

Ansley's mom spoke up first saying, "Well, I think you need to ask Vet Julie if she wants to go."

Vet Julie looked at the girls and said, "That sounds like it would be fun, so let's do it."

They finished their lemonade and walked down to the river bank and climbed into their kayaks.

Vet Julie looked around said, "Wow, what a beautiful spot on the river. The water is so clear and calm. This would be a beautiful painting."

Ansley replied, "Yes, we really love it here."

Rosie interrupted saying, "We had better hurry before it gets dark."

They quickly paddled to the island and pulled their kayaks onto the bank. Ansley and Rosie started walking toward the other side of the island.

Vet Julie asked, "So girls, what kind of treasure do you think we will find?"

Ansley answered, "Necklaces, rings, Indian arrow heads, lawn chairs to name a few. You name it we have probably found it."

Rosie added, "Yes and sometimes we find things that are alive. Like snakes and fish and lizards."

Ansley suddenly stopped walking and said, "Vet Julie, we have a problem."

"What's the problem?" asked Vet Julie.

"Well," started Ansley. "Can you keep a secret Vet Julie and will you pinkie swear to not tell anyone?"

"Ok, you have my attention," replied Vet Julie. "What have you girls found? Gold?"

Rosie quickly answered, "I guess you might say it's better than gold."

Vet Julie was really curious now, "Well, is it a treasure map?"

Ansley took her hand and said, "Let's slide into this hole and you'll see soon enough."

Ansley grabbed the stash of flashlights and slide down into the hole. Vet Julie and Rosie was right behind her. They turned on their flashlights and started looking around. Vet Julie held out her flashlight and looked around. She saw what looked like a fish tail. She slowly moved her flashlight along the tail and saw a female human torso. She jumped back and turned to the girls.

"That's a good one, you got me. I thought it was real there for a moment," laughed Vet Julie. "Where did you get it or did you make it?"

"No, she's real and she's hurt," insisted Ansley. "That's why we need you. You've got to help her."

Vet Julie took a step closer and the mermaid slide back against the wall.

Vet Julie just stood there in astonishment and finally said, "Oh my goodness she is real. Oh my, oh my."

The mermaid was looking at them with big wide eyes and suddenly let out a squeal that pierced their ears.

After everyone calmed down, Vet Julie asked, "Where is she hurt?"

Ansley answered, "Look, it's her arm. See where we bandaged it."

Rosie added, "It's all red and oozing."

As Vet Julie inched closer Ansley tells the mermaid, "It's ok, this is Vet Julie and she's here to help."

Ansley gently picked up the mermaid's arm. Vet Julie moved closer and shined her flashlight on the mermaid's arm. "Yes, that looks pretty bad. I wonder how that happened?"

"Well, I think when it flooded," answered Ansley. "When I was swept away in the flood something pushed me up on a rock. I know now it was the mermaid who saved me and Lucky Dog."

"Well girls, I will need to go to my truck and get some supplies," said Vet Julie.

"No! Mom will see you," insisted Ansley.

"You mean your mom doesn't know?" questioned Vet Julie.

"No, she doesn't know," answered Ansley.

Rosie added, "We're afraid if anyone finds out they will take her away and keep her in a cage."

Vet Julie looked at them and said, "Girls, I can't treat her unless I get my supplies and we will need clean buckets of water. This is so unreal I still can't believe it."

The mermaid was looking at them and her eyelids were getting droopy and her eyes seemed to be growing weak.

Ansley was getting more concerned by the minute and said, "Ok, lets head back to the house, she doesn't look so good."

When they got back to the house, Toots was sitting out on the porch so they joined her.

Vet Julie said, "Toots, I need you to listen."

"Ok, this sounds serious," replied Toots. "What did you all find?"

Vet Julie replied, "It looks like the girls have found a treasure."

Toots very proudly said, "I know, they have lots of treasures."

Vet Julie very seriously said, "Yes, but this one is very unique and we must keep it a secret that no one else can know."

Ansley and Rosie both said at the same time, "Yes, no one else can know."

Toots was getting more curious and asked, "What kind of treasure did you girls find?"

"Well, I think seeing is believing."

"Ok I think you all want me to go see for myself. Am I right?"

"Yes," answered Vet Julie, "But first I need to go get my supplies from the truck and you girls get some jugs of clean water."

Vet Julie went to the truck while the girls filled some jugs with water. In the meantime, Toots gets her kayak and dragged it to the river bank.

When they were getting in their kayaks Toots said, "This had better be good."

Ansley and Rosie both said at the same time, "Oh it is. You just wait and see."

They paddled to the island in silence. They gathered up their water and supplies and walked to the entrance to the hole.

Ansley handed her mom a flashlight and Toots looked down and said, "I'm not getting in that hole. What do you girls have in there that you can't bring out?"

Ansley said, "Mom, you will just have to go in and see."

Toots was still not sold on the idea and said, "You know I don't like caves."

Ansley replied, "Mom, it's not a small space when you get down there. You can stand up just like a room."

Toots hesitated and said, "I think I will just wait here."

Rosie pointed to a nice flat spot at the edge of the hole and said, "Ok, sit here" and Toots sat down.

Ansley and Rosie get ready to go after Vet Julie had already slide down. Then Ansley and Rosie slide down and   turned around and they each grabbed one of Toot's legs and gave a tug.

She came sliding down the hole screaming, "Girls let me go," and they did.

By the time Toots was sitting on the bottom of the cave floor, she was still gripping the flashlight that Ansley had given her. She stood up, turned it on and looked where Vet Julie was kneeling down. She saw the mermaid and started screaming again.

This time it was, "What is that!"

Ansley calmly said, "Mom, quit screaming. You are scaring her."

"Scaring what?" ask Toots.

"The mermaid," whispered Rosie.

"The what? Say that again," stuttered Toots.

"The mermaid," said Ansley, Rosie, and Vet Julie at the same time.

Ansley took her mom's hand and said, "Mom, you don't look so good. Maybe you should sit down.

"No, I'm ok. Is she alive?" asked Toots.

"Yes, she is," answered Vet Julie, "But her arm is badly infected and I need to get started on trying to get it cleaned up. First, we need to let her know that I going to help her. Can we make her understand what I am going to do?"

Ansley held her right arm out and pointed to the mermaid's arm. Then Ansley asked Vet Julie, "Will you clean my arm and then apply the dressing so the mermaid can see what you are going to do?"

So Vet Julie cleaned and wrapped Ansley's right arm.

The mermaid watched everything that Vet Julie did to Ansley. Then Ansley very gently touched the mermaid's arm and she flinched and pulled it back. Ansley touched it again and this time the mermaid slowly lifted her arm up. Vet Julie slowly and gently cleaned the mermaid's arm and then applied a nice clean bandage.

Vet Julie looked at the girls and said, "Now, I need to give her a shot of antibiotics."

"Good luck with that," shrugged Rosie, "I hate shots."

Vet Julie got out her needle and filled it with antibiotics. She started to pick up the mermaid's left arm and the mermaid started swinging it.

Vet Julie thought for a minute and said, "Well, I guess giving her a shot isn't going to work. What has she been eating?"

Ansley replied, "Apples, bananas, cookies, tuna fish, and things like that."

"Mmmmm, so is that what happened to my tuna fish," asked Ansley's mom.

"Yes, and she loved it," answered Rosie.

"Well, that's good. We can give her an antibiotic pill in the tuna three times a day," replied Vet Julie.

"Wow, that's a lot of tuna," murmured Ansley, "We'll have to stock up."

Vet Julie thought for a minute and said, Yyou girls will have to keep her top warm and I see her tail is in the water. That's good. Here Ansley give her this pill in a can of tuna."

"Ok, I will," replied Ansley.

Ansley and Rosie tell the mermaid goodbye and they will see her in the morning.

They all climbed out of the hole and walked to their kayaks in silence. They get in and paddled back across the river. They dragged the kayaks onto the bank and walked up the path to the house. They went inside and washed up for dinner. They sat down at the dining room table and said their prayers. For Rosie's parents, for the rescue workers, for Lucky Dog, and for the mermaid.

As they ate their dinner the main topic of conversation was the importance of not telling anyone about the mermaid.

"If anyone outside of this group knows, they will come and trap the mermaid and put her in a place to study her or run tests and take blood samples and she will never see freedom again," cautioned Vet Julie.

"We know," said Ansley and Rosie.

"Well then, we all know to keep this a secret to ourselves," added Ansley's mom.

Ansley and Rosie looked at each other and right then and there they pinkie swore to keep the mermaid a secret.

Vet Julie Thanked them for inviting her to dinner, the campfire and the s'mores and especially for letting her know about the mermaid.

As she was leaving, she said, "Oh and by the way Lucky Dog will probably be able to come home in another day or two."

Toots, Ansley, and Rosie at the same time cheered, "That's great news."

Chapter 17

Every morning the girls wake up, hurry and do their chores and go to the island to check on and feed the mermaid. One morning about a week later, they go to the island, slide down the hole, and to their surprise, no mermaid.

"Oh no! Where did she go?" exclaimed Rosie!

They looked everywhere and then climbed back out of the hole. They looked around but didn't see any sign of her.

"Where is she?" shouted Ansley.

"I don't know," answered Rosie. "Maybe over there under those bushes."

They both went running and crawled under the bushes but she wasn't there.

Ansley thought for a moment and said, "Let's walk all the way around the island checking along the edge of the water."

They did that and didn't see the mermaid anywhere.

"What now?" asked Rosie.

"Let's go get our kayaks and go down the river," suggested Ansley.

Just as they were getting in their kayaks, they heard the porch bell ringing so they paddled toward the house.

Ansley and Rosie hopped out and tied up their kayaks and walked up to the porch.

Ansley asked, "What's up Mom?"

Toots had the truck keys in her hand and she said, "Vet Julie called to let us know that we can pick up Lucky Dog."

Both girls shouted, "That's great, let's go."

As they were driving into town Ansley said, "Mom, the mermaid is gone."

Her mom replied, "What do you mean, 'gone'?"

Ansley answered, "Well, like we can't find her gone."

Rosie added, "Yes gone. We searched the whole island and we were getting ready to search down and up the river when you rang the bell."

"Well," said Toots, "All we can do is hope that we see her again or accept the fact that she is well enough to go back to where she was before the flood."

Both girls sat in silence with their heads bowed in sadness until Rosie looked up and said, "Just maybe she likes it here and will stay around."

"The chances of that happening are slim, but one can hope," said Ansley's mom.

As they pulled up there stood Vet Julie and Lucky Dog. Lucky Dog took a few steps to meet them.

"Look," cried Ansley, "He's getting around on three legs."

They jumped out of the truck and ran over to hug Lucky Dog. His tail is wagging a mile a minute.

"Oh boy Lucky Dog, I'm soooo glad we can finally take you home," said Ansley as she leaned over to hug him again.

"Me too," added Rosie as she hugged him too.

Toots, Ansley, and Rosie are all taking turns hugging Lucky Dog.

Vet Julie squatted down to join them and said, "His leg is almost healed. Keep him in a fenced in area for now, give him these meds once a day, change the dressing every other day and bring him back a week from today for a checkup."

They helped Lucky Dog into the truck and Ansley whispered to Vet Julie, "The mermaid is gone. We couldn't find her anywhere this morning."

"Maybe she'll turn up. I wouldn't give up hope," said Vet Julie.

"Speaking of hope," added Vet Julie, "Any word on the search?"

"No," answered Toots, "But Don is supposed to call tonight. We aren't giving up hope."

"No, we are not," added Rosie as tears rolled down her face.

They all climbed in to the truck and waved bye to Vet Julie as Toots started the truck.

"Thank you," shouted Ansley.

"You are welcome," shouted Vet Julie. "See you soon."

Chapter 18

When they get back home, the first thing they did was unload Lucky Dog.

"Easy boy, we will lift you down."

They put him into the side yard that was fenced in and there was a nice doghouse. They got him a fresh bowl of water and some food.

"He'll be nice and cozy and safe here," Ansley's mom assured them.

The girls sat and watched Lucky Dog as he walked around checking out the fence.

Ansley told him, "We have to keep you safe and in here until your leg heels and you are getting around a little bit better."

They gave him a big hug and went through the gate. They closed it behind them and headed up on to the porch.

Toots came out and said, "Come on girls, let's eat our lunch and then we will go for a swim in the river."

They finished eating their lunch, quickly cleaned up their dishes, and started toward the river.

Ansley stopped and said, "Mom, can we go to the island and check to see if the mermaid is there first?"

"Sure," answered Ansley's mom.

The girls went running and quickly paddled to the island to check on the mermaid. They slid down the hole and no mermaid.

They called, "Hello, hello." They climbed back out and shouted,

"Hello, helloooo."

All they heard was their echo and Ansley said, "That's it, we will call her Echo so when we shout for her people will think we are just echoing our voice."

"Sounds great," agreed Rosie.

So, they both walked around shouting, "Echo, Echo, Echoooo."

There was no sign of the mermaid. The girls got in their kayaks and paddled back across the river.

They grabbed their tubes and Ansley hollered, "Come on, let's float to the golden hole and swim there where the water is deeper."

Her mom hollered back, "Wait girls, I'm coming too."

They put their tubes in the water, climbed on, and relaxed as they started floating toward the golden hole. It was so amazing to lay back and watch the white clouds dotting the blue sky and smell the sweet scents of the wild flowers growing along the banks of the river.

"What an absolutely beautiful day," murmured Ansley's mom.

"It would be better if we could find Echo," added Ansley.

"What's echo?" asked Ansley's mom.

Both girls laughed at the same time, "It's the mermaid."

"Echo, why Echo?" asked Ansley's mom.

"So, when we call for her, everyone will think we are just echoing our voice," answered Ansley.

"Oh, that's a good idea," agreed her mom.

They all started shouting, "Echo, Echo" and they heard, "Echooo, Echooooo." They arrived at the golden hole and tossed their tubes up on the bank.

They swam around playing and shouting, "Marco Polo, Marco Polo."

All at once Rosie asked, "Are there fish in here?"

"Yes," answered Ansley, "I caught a big one a while back."

Rosie exclaimed, "Something just hit my leg."

Ansley excitedly said, "Mine too" and at that very moment she went falling backwards and her head went under the water. She came jumping up spitting water and demanded, "Why did you do that?"

Rosie just looked at her and said, "Do what?"

Ansley said, "You know what. You hit my leg and made me go under the water."

Rosie still just looked at her and said, "I didn't. How could I have hit your leg when I'm right here in front of you?"

At that very moment, Ansley's mom cried, "Hey, what's happening?"

The girls looked over and Toots was going under the water. The next minute her head was coming up from under the water.

"Mom, are you ok?" cried Ansley.

To their astonishment, Toots comes on up and out of the water and she's sitting on the mermaid's back. The mermaid goes back down under the water and Toots rolls off.

She comes sputtering back up out of the water and said, "Well, now we know where the mermaid is."

They look across the river and the mermaid was perched up on a log.

Ansley swam over to her and said, "Let me see your arm," and Ansley pointed to her arm. "Wow, it looks a whole lot better," murmured Ansley.

Then she noticed that there was something sticky on the mermaid's arm and when she looked closer, she realized that it was honey. By that time her mom and Rosie had swam over also.

Ansley looked at her mom and Rosie and said, "Look, her arm looks so much better and she has been putting honey on it. Where do you think she got the honey?"

Toots thought for a minute and then said, "Well, farmer Workman has some bee hives down river from here. He cleans the hives in the river after he has removed the honey. I'll bet that's where she got the honey."

The mermaid slid off the log and went under the water. They watched to see where she would come up. All of a sudden, they got water splashed in their faces when the mermaid flapped her tail in the water.

"Help, I can't see," laughed Rosie.

"Me either," added Ansley.

They all giggled and swam around. Going under the water and back up. The mermaid started doing what they were doing. The mermaid swam up to Ansley and turned around. Ansley put her arms around the mermaid's neck and was lying on the mermaid's back.

The mermaid took off swimming around and Ansley sat up and started yelling, "Yee-hi" as the mermaid started diving under the water and coming back up.

Ansley's mom called, "Hold on."

The mermaid went down under the water in the middle of the golden hole and she went to the very bottom. Ansley couldn't hold her breath any longer and she let go of the mermaid. She swam to the surface and came up coughing.

The mermaid came up beside her and Ansley looked at her and said, "Obviously I can't hold my breath as long as you can."

Rosie wondered out loud, "I wonder how long the mermaid can hold her breath?"

"Well," says Ansley's mom, "She is part fish so maybe her lungs are more like a fish and she can stay under the water longer like a fish or something." Toots realized it was getting late so she said, "Come on girls we had better get ready to go."

Toots, Ansley, and Rosie reluctantly got out of the water and dried off. They gathered up their tubes and started walking back up the river trail toward home. As they walked along talking about the adventure they had just experienced, they kept their eyes on the river and every now and then they would spot the mermaid's tail.

Ansley said, "I sure hope no one else finds her."

"Me too," added Rosie.

Toots added, "Girls, I think she knows to keep out of sight and I think she can sense when people are around."

All of a sudden, Ansley said, "Race you" and took off running.

Rosie took off right behind her.

Toots just kept walking her steady pace and said, "Girls, I'm going to enjoy the rest of my walk and take time to enjoy the view and smell the roses."

Chapter 19

That afternoon as they were planning dinner the phone rang. Ansley answered the phone and said, "Hello."

Then she heard, "Hey girl, it's your daddy."

She jumped up and down in delight and then asked, "Dad, oh Dad, I'm so glad to hear your voice. Where are you?"

He replied, "I'm at the airport. Will you tell your mom to start-up the van and bring it to the airport to get me?"

Ansley couldn't stop chattering, "OK! OK!." She hung up the phone and announced, "That was Dad and he's here."

Her mom replied, "What, what do you mean? Where? Where is he?"

Ansley said, "He's at the airport."

Her mom still didn't quite get it and asked, "Our airport?"

Ansley replied, "Yes, our airport and he wants you to come and get him."

Toots said, "Well, come on, let's go."

They quickly put on their shoes and Toots grabbed the truck keys.

Ansley noticed and said, "Mom, Dad said to bring the van."

Toots said, "Ok" and they ran out to get in the van.

They were so excited and then Rosie stopped right before getting in the van and started crying.

In between sobs, she said, "I guess Mom and Dad didn't make it."

Ansley and her mom stopped as they thought about that possibility.

Then Aunt Toots said, "Rosie dear, if they haven't found them yet, it doesn't mean they won't. I'm sure they are still looking. Your Uncle Don probably came home to check on things here. It's time to take some of the yearlings to the cattle market and there is still some fence mending that has to be finished before winter comes."

They all settled down and got in the van. They were all quiet on the way to the airport. Each one lost in their own thoughts.

Just as Toots pulled in a parking space at the airport, her cell phone rang. She answered, "Hello, yes Don. Where are you? Ok, we'll be there in a minute." She turned to Ansley and Rosie and said, "He's at Gate 2."

They went in the front main entrance and ran to Gate 2 and there stood Ansley's dad with his suitcase. They all ran over and hugged him.

Rosie sniffled, "Uncle Don, what about Mom and Dad?"

He looked at her with gentleness and said, "Rosie, we looked and searched and searched and looked some more. But if you will turn around, you can ask them whatever you want to yourself."

Rosie turned around and there stood her dad on crutches and her mom had a sling on her left arm. Rosie ran crying and hugged them so hard her dad almost lost his balance.

Ansley joined them and said, "Group family hug."

So her parents came over and they were all hugging and crying and hugging even tighter.

Don said, "Family hugs are the best."

Rosie's dad Jack agreed, "Yes, they are."

They finished hugging and gathered all the luggage and everyone got settled in the van after they helped Jack get settled in.

Toots said, "Rosie, we all prayed for this moment, we had faith in the search team and that it would happen. We had faith and we believed that your parents would be found. Let's all thank God for His guidance during this trying time."

The drive home was totally different than the drive to the airport.

Don asked, "So girls, how are things on the farm?"

Ansley answered, "Actually Dad, you might not believe it but everything is fine. Some things are better and some things are different."

"Different?" questioned her dad.

"You'll just have to wait and see Dad," was all that Ansley would say so they talked about keeping up with the chores and how well Lucky Dog was doing with just three legs.

Chapter 20

That evening at dinner Rosie's parents, Jack and Marie, told them about what had happened. First one engine had stopped working when it overheated. Then the second engine wasn't powerful enough to get them back to shore in the raging water and it overheated also. The captain was afraid that the boat was going to capsize so everyone had to put on their lifejackets and jump overboard. Some people were able to get in the lifeboats but some of the boats had already been swept away in the storm. Then Don told them about how the search team had spent days circling back and forth combing every inch of water and the many scattered small islands but always remaining hopeful.

They finally caught a break when they found debris on a remote island and some life jackets piled on the top. The funny part was neither of her parents got hurt in the actual storm. Marie told them how they had been lucky landing on an island that had plenty of food to survive on but she fell when she was climbing a banana tree to get some bananas and broke her arm. Then Jack told his story about how they had seen the rescuers in the distance a few days earlier and he took off running to climb the cliffs to light the signal fire on the top. He got about halfway up and some rocks gave way and he fell.

He looked around and said, "It is so good to be home."

Rosie said, "I'm just glad you are both home."

Don stood up and said, "We are all thankful. Now Toots, how are things here on the farm?"

She replied, "Everything is doing great; the cattle are ready for market."

Don praised them saying, "Good job girls, I'll take them in the morning."

Ansley was curious and asked her dad, "How many didn't survive the boat wreck?"

Her dad thought for a minute and finally answered, "Ansley, we only talk about the ones we save and we pray for the ones we didn't?"

Then Ansley suggested, "How about we all go out for a campfire where we can relax and talk some more?"

Ansley's dad laughed and replied, "That sounds like a great idea since your Uncle Jack didn't get to build his fire, we'll let him help build this one."

"Ha, ha, I'll let you all do it this time until I can get around a little bit better," he laughed.

They had just settled down around the campfire when Lucky Dog came hopping over.

Don leaned over to hug him and said, "It's so good to see you boy," and Lucky's tail was wagging in obvious joy.

They were all relaxed sitting back in their chairs and eating their s'mores. All at once, Don sat up a little straighter in his chair as something caught his attention. His eyes skim up and down over the river as he could see something moving around out there.

Ansley could see the question on his face as he said, "What in the world is going on here? What is that?"

Without hesitation, Ansley said, "It's the mermaid. She's the one that has been going up and down the river finding things of value and putting them on the island. That's how I found the necklace which by the way was worth five thousand dollars."

Don said in wonderment, "A mermaid?"

"Yes, it's true," replied Ansley, her mom, and Rosie in unison.

Don got up and walked to the edge of the river with Lucky Dog right beside him.

He turned around and asked them, "So why isn't she afraid and swimming away?"

Ansley walked down beside her dad and answered, "Because she is used to us and she did save me and Lucky Dog. We figure she has been around for a while and has been watching us long before the flood. Her arm was hurt and we think she got hurt saving us and we helped nurse her. Also, she was wearing one of my swim tops that came up missing last year."

Ansley's mom joined them and said, "Echo is our secret and no one can know. We can't tell anyone else."

"Well," started Don, "The old timers have talked about seeing a big fish tail in the river for years. So is she a legend or a myth?"

Ansley replied, "That's easy. She's neither. she's real."

They all agree it would be best to not tell anyone else. They made a pact that night and to this day they have kept it. If you ask any of them anything about a mermaid, they will laugh and ask you if you have been in the sun too long. So, what do you think? Is she a legend or a myth or the best kept secret in Greenbrier County, West Virginia?